Those Necessary Thorns:
Sex &
Decadence

Sabrina Childress

Those Necessary Thorns: Sex & Decadence

For information regarding special discounts for bulk purchases, please visit Those Necessary Thorns at www.TNTBook.com or email Books@CandMConcepts

First Edition: March 2015

Printed in the United States of America

ISBN: 978-0-9960669-1-4

C & M Concepts Presents

What If....

For information regarding special discounts for bulk purchases, please visit www.TNTBook.com

First Edition: January 2015

Printed in the United States of America

IBSN: 978-0-9960669-3-8

DEDICATION

I would like to dedicate this book to so many and so few. So in the interest of time I will go with the few. To Malcolm Davis, I am forever grateful that we met! Call it divine order! To Jonathan Hood you are the voice behind the mic and I thank you for your unwavering support! To my Just Talkin' ladies, Kneeasha, Leeza, Varielle, Kamari, and Destiny, I love you dearly! You are my inspiration to keep going! To my first lady, Rita Richardson, nothing but smiles and love to you my dear! Thank you for the encouragement and steadfast belief in me! To my twin, Tracey, you already know what it is!

And finally, to my readers, thank you for embracing my words and coming back for more! All of the letters, emails, and social media love has been nothing short of tremendous.

As always, an enormous thanks to all who are reading this acknowledgement, and will call me later to ask why I didn't mention them. No worries, I'm protecting you. You're welcome!

CONTENTS

ACKNOWLEDGMENTS

To Marcelena Ordaz, the editor of this creation and friend for life, to whom I am indebted. It took forever to find you again and I will never let us get lost again.

To J. Will, always and forever and there is no changing that. Your talents are many and your success is there for the taking!

0
BANG

As the sunrise inched its way into the morning sky, the six foot two inch, muscular, mulatto male frame shifted restlessly on the leather of the driver's seat. Behind limo tinted windows he watched the front door of a framed house with malicious intent. His eyes ablaze with anger and his face filled with hurt. He watched a smiling Desiree waving goodbye to the man at the door, back out of the driveway onto the residential street, and disappeared. His eyes narrowed when the door finally closed and his target moved away from the window.

An exhausted James Jones Taylor had followed me to this house and waited all night for me to leave. He could feel his heart pounding in his ears as he marched up the walkway, rang the doorbell, and quickly moved out of sight. The door opened and the seriousness of the situation became all too real. A shirtless, Raymond Humphrey was barefoot and wearing nothing but a pair of black cotton pajama bottoms. He held his hands up and slowly backed away from the barrel of the gun.

"Listen, you don't want to do this."

"Yes I do." James said with fire in his eyes.

"It's not what you think." Ray said keeping his eyes locked on James' trigger finger.

"Save it you sorry son of a bitch!" James said pressing his way forward into Ray's foyer. As he navigated his way into the house he noticed the enormous canvass painting out the corner of his eye. "What the fuck is that?"

Ray looked up at a wide eyed James and then over at the painting. "It's nothing. Just some art."

"That's Desiree! That's my wife!" James shouted in disbelief. "How long have you been fucking my wife?!" The rage in the center of his body began to boil over and spill out into his words.

"That's what I'm trying to tell you! We aren't fucking. I'm in love with her, yes, but fucking her no. She was here because she is a good woman and wanted me to know that she is yours," Ray said almost babbling. "This whole thing was a set up that didn't go as planned."

"What the fuck do you mean set up?" James said cocking the gun. "By who?"

"You're boy Wesley, that's who!" Ray confessed. "I just got hip to it myself. The only problem is he couldn't control the variables – that's us man."

"How do you know Wes?"

"He was a friend." Ray looked down at the gun and tried to figure a way out of the life and death situation suddenly in front of him.

"I should kill you where you stand!" James said slightly lowering the piece of steel.

"Why? What will that solve?" Ray asked in an attempt to temper the situation.

"It would mean payback is a bitch," James said sternly. *BANG!* James fired a single shot into Ray's thigh.

"Fuuuuuuucccccckkkkkkkk!!!!!!" Ray screamed and grabbed his leg.

"Now I feel a little better," James said walking over to where Ray had fallen. "You silly muthafuckas think you're so goddamned slick. But I appreciate you confirming what I already knew," James said tapping Ray's cheek.

As Ray writhed in pain on the floor, James walked over to the mantle where the gigantic painting of his wife rested. He took a moment to stare at the features of the face when he felt his eyes water. James pulled the painting off the mantle and knocked it to the ground. The large wooden frame that held its contents gave way with a crack as the image landed face up. There they were, my big brown eyes staring up at him. James stood over the painting and focused on my face. He raised his leg in an attempt to deface the image but found himself feeling a wave of guilt and remorse. The chain of events that led to this very moment didn't seem this big or this drastic. *It was one simple mistake. One.* He thought to himself. Who knew all of this would be the end result.

James turned to find Raymond had moved toward the door. He quickly regained his composure and hurried to stop him. "Look, I love my wife. I would do anything for her. *Anything* to keep my family together," James said waving the gun. Ray paused to assess his means of escape.

"I can understand that but this is not about her. Right now I need to get to a hospital and fast."

"Trust me you will."

"I don't mean in a body bag."

"That remains to be seen," J.J. said snidely as he knelt down to peer into the eyes of his prey. "That would be too easy. I'm the type of man that likes to watch the suffering."

"You *are* crazy!" Raymond asserted.

"Isn't everybody a little crazy?" J.J. said with a raised brow and a smirk.

"Let's stop playing games! Wesley is the one that had it out for you from the very beginning."

"Explain." James said curiously, pointing the loaded gun at Raymond's side.

1
CLICHES FOR ROSES

"If fire breaks out and catches in thorns so that the stacked grain or the standing grain or the field is consumed, he who started the fire shall make full restitution." Exodus 22:6

After James and I left church that faithful afternoon we went home and had a long talk. The things that happened between J.J. and I brought out another side of him. He was more attentive and spontaneous and even wilder in the sack. After a brief stent at church-based couple's therapy we agreed the trust in our relationship was broken but not beyond repair. Reconnecting as individuals was going to be the best way to bring us back together. But after having a taste of Ray I knew I wanted – no needed more from J.J. I'd wondered if he'd ever considered role-playing or swinging, so I asked. We laughed it off awkwardly. I think I was more interested in the idea than J.J. but was too scared to admit it. My Ray days are long over but his special brand of touch was long overdue. He'd contacted me a few times but I never responded. James and I believed it was best for us – well me – to take some time to regroup. We spoke about it in great detail. We decided that I needed space and time to get myself together, so I moved out because all I did was replay everything in my mind daily. It was time to change the situation and scenery, so I found a small place, changed my mind, and then relocated once more to a larger more comfy place. So here I am.

My name is still Desiree Elizabeth Taylor and that's about the only thing I can say is still the same about me. A lot has changed for me. My troubles are gone, although oddly enough, I think I miss them sometimes. All of the excitement has died down and my life has somewhat returned to normal. It's been a long road, but here I am. Here we are, being normal again: *Whatever that is.*

I'm not proud of the things I went through to get here. Not to mention, these scars are constant reminders of the things that went horribly wrong in my life. I touch them, dream about them, revisit them and cry for them. I hadn't fully understood the magnitude of the situation that I'd gotten myself into. As my fingers swayed back and forth over my belly, I imagined the physical scars on my body, making an ugly braille pattern that, in my mind, spelled *helpless*. These things I'd done to myself, I own them. I own my part in all of it. It's time to come clean about these scars. I can't get a good night's sleep for all the things and memories that haunt me. I needed my life to be less complicated...less cluttered.

I lay in the bed that evening trying to imagine what kind of mother I would be -- would have been. I was almost appalled by my lack of emotional connection to it all. I should have been feeling something sad or demoralizing, right? Well I didn't. I felt absolutely nothing. It was the kind of nothing feeling you get trying to feel bad for a piece of candy dropped on the floor.

I must be a monster. I thought, as I moved my fingers across the scars on my belly. I tried to imagine what being ripped open felt like. Think about it, child birth is and always will be a life and death situation. Except in my case, I'd decided I was going to determine my own outcome. In that moment I consciously chose death and now in this moment I'm consciously choosing life. I'm sure GOD will deal with me on judgment day, but in the meantime, I will do what I have to do to get back in HIS good graces. The first step to getting back to life was to simply start by feeling again. Easier said than done, but totally doable...I think.

For months I've been going through some spiritual pain of my own. I couldn't rub these scars away. I couldn't stop thinking about who helped cause them all of those months ago; Raymond Humphrey and James Jones Taylor. When I needed him he wasn't there. I would've given my life for him. *Hell*, I almost did in more ways than one. *"I love you in a place where there is no space or time,"* I hummed in an out of key melody. In the back of my mind, I really thought we'd come back together one more time.

There's a cliché that says no man is an island; well this woman is. For most people this loud silence would be deafening, but in this case it was the greatest sound in the world. One thing was for sure, no one would be ringing my line -- not even my infamous girl crew; Sasha, Tara, Angel, Trisha, Kim and definitely *not* Tina! After the fiasco, I changed my number. When I moved I left no forwarding address for anyone who wasn't of real importance. I took a leave of absence from work so I could make sense of all that had taken place without interruption. This was a solo mission that required such extreme actions. Not everyone is privileged enough to do something so drastic for this type of healing, but I was eternally grateful that I'd created a world where this option was possible.

I usually consider myself a pretty emotionally strong and stable person. Let's be realistic, we've all been through things and we've all got our extremes but I'd always considered matters of the heart to be small by comparison. Guess I was wrong. With such a sobering thought, I untangled myself from the blankets and crawled toward the end of the bed. First things first, get up and say a prayer for my sanity, then make a to-do-list.

Just after sunset, I sat on a cushioned wicker chair at my brown woven table, on the balcony of my new place with a bottle of champagne, orange juice and a glass, overlooking the water. All of the yachts seemed to form a smiley face. I smiled back at them and all was at peace. It wasn't easy getting here. I turned to my left and peered through the clear sliding glass doors at the boxes lying in wait scattered about my safe haven. I was in no hurry to unpack anything except the glasses, other dishes and cookware. Cooking always seemed to calm me while simultaneously providing a nice distraction from whatever was going on in my world. I popped the bottle of champagne and poured my first glass. I added the orange juice and sipped my mimosa with deliberate intent and thought about sex and decadence as I watched the world go by while I wrote;

Randomness of an Intelligent Woman

I thought I was smarter than this!
I knew that I knew better but I kissed a fool
and now my heart can't take the consequences.

I hate the fact that I miss him so much!
I hate the fact that I want to tell him that I
miss him so much!
I hate the fact that he wasn't ready for me or
my love....
And I...wasn't ready for him.

I thought I was smarter than this!
I knew that I knew better but I kissed a fool
and now my heart can't take the consequences.

At some point I know it will get better
At some point....
At some point....
My tears will get better....
At some point.

My heart won't sink every time I see his
face.
My hair won't gray every time he walks
away.
My eyes won't water on a sunny day.
And my heart won't reach for him....all
because I took it away.

I thought I was smarter than this!

*I knew that I knew better but I kissed a fool
and now my heart can't take the consequences.*

*The randomness of an intelligent
woman....Go figure!*

They say once a good girl has gone, she's
gone forever. I'm not sure how true that is, however,
I do know I've plummeted into the dark side and
came back changed forever. So I guess there is
some truth to it. Now all that's left is to see which
side I favor most.

2
OUTSIDER

The one and only Mr. Raymond Humphrey stood just across a pile of dirt from me. It seemed like such a fitting metaphor, if you think about it. There he stood, tall, chocolate, deep-voiced and wearing a bluish-gray suit, white shirt, multi-colored tie, solid gray fedora complete with a black accent strip and feather, white and blue handkerchief and sunglasses hanging from the pocket of his suit jacket, stealing glances at me from time to time. At each of his attempts to approach me, I'd move away or began a conversation with someone else.

By request of the last client we shared, we were front and center at their ground-breaking ceremony poised and ready for any pictures, questions, and congratulatory handshakes. It was extremely hard to ensure my facial expressions cooperated with my mind instead of my emotions, but somehow I managed to pull it off. This man...this fine, well-put-together man, who'd proclaimed his love for me amidst all of the chaos, was within arm's reach of me and all I could do to prevent myself from crying was shake hands and move around the crowd to avoid him at all costs.

I'd overheard him telling an investor how

remarkable it was to work with me and that I was a major part of pulling all of this together. Ray pointed me out, "You see that beautiful angel over there, dressed in the all white dress, red belt, red heels with the feathered hair? She's the one we should all thank for pulling *and* keeping this project together, on track, and under budget."
I turned to nod and smile in their direction and picked up a glass of champagne from the waiter passing by.

"High praise is needed indeed," the investor responded, raising his glass in my direction. "And I'm sure it didn't hurt that she is a very attractive woman either," he said with a wink and a smile at Ray.

"No, that didn't hurt at all," he said looking in my direction and thinking, *"She definitely doesn't look pregnant, that's for sure."* We'd seen each other on more than one occasion out and about either alone or with friends. I'd noticed him once or twice, but never acknowledged him in a definitive way. Just like today, our eyes would meet and one of us would turn away.

After a few hours of socializing, Ray concluded a conversation then looked around for any resemblance of me when he noticed I'd slipped away without saying goodbye. So, he did the next best thing; he called my best friend for an update. Ray dialed Tina's phone number and took a stroll around the property.

"Hey stranger!" Ray said, trying not to sound suspicious. "It's been a long time."

"What do you want Ray?" Tina snapped.

"*Wooow!* Hold on, why all the attitude old friend?" he asked quickly.

"Friend?! So now we're friends? I haven't heard from you since our last little play date. No phone calls. No emails. No text messages. Nothing!" Tina reminded him.

"I know. I know. I've just been really busy and time got away from me. You know how it is," he explained nonchalantly. Even though he honestly felt like he didn't owe Tina any explanation, he provided a miniscule one.

"What, I wasn't fun anymore?" Tina asked ashamed.

"No, it wasn't that...it's just...I had a lot of figuring out to do. Things were getting crazy. My girl said you got hurt in a fight or something so I thought it would be best to cool it for a while. You're a lot wilder than I thought," he said with a laugh.

"*Soooo,* shouldn't you have called to check on me? I thought we had something special."

"We did. Sex! It was fun while it lasted," Ray said coldly.

"Oh, I see!"

"Why are you acting like that?"

"Like what?"

"You did know what that was, didn't you?"

"Loud and clear."

"Okay. Hey, I was wondering...how's Desiree these days?" he asked slyly but Tina didn't answer. "I thought I saw here the other day," Ray said, turning to look for me in the distance.

"That's why you called me?"

"No," he said quickly. "I called because I was wondering how you're doing and the conversation was getting cold so I changed the subject. Why are you so damn hostile anyway, she *is* your best friend."

Tina realized that Ray had no idea about what transpired between her and Desi. She smiled and answered, "Desiree is doing just fine."

"Oh, well that's good," he answered somewhat disappointed. "Tell her I said hello the next time you see her."

"Will do, Mr. Humphrey. Anything else?"

"Yes, don't be a stranger. The phone works both ways."

"Goodbye Mr. Humphrey," Tina hung up the phone.

Ray looked at his phone and placed it back into his jacket pocket. *"My Desiree. My sweet, sweet Desiree!"* he thought to himself. *"It's been way too long since the last time she was in my arms. I've never in my life loved a woman so much and despised her for the same feeling at the same time. I've tried every trick in the book to get over her, but nothing, and I do mean nothing has cured me. I can't stop thinking about her. Whoever said time heals all wounds lied! I mean completely fabricated that whole idea!"*

3
FRIENDS AND ENEMIES

Tina allowed the fingers of one hand to glide along the crimson and gold accented wall as she steadied herself, while the other hand gripped the base of a large wine glass. She walked down the side-saddled flight of stairs, which for decorative purposes was missing the handrail and instead lined with large glittery gold block unlit candles every other step leading to her cellar. Once she reached the bottom, she glanced at the jumbo furry throw pillows strategically placed in the space directly behind the stairwell, then continued her drunken walk around the counter and finally stopped when she landed behind the marble accented bar. Girl X followed behind her shortly thereafter. Both ladies were dressed comfortably in snug jeans and fitted dress shirts that showed off more curves than Jessica Rabbit. Tina allowed her breasts to heave forward and out by releasing the first three buttons on the v-neck blouse, while her company only allowed them to breathe slightly through a sheer blouse. The tight bun in Girl X's hair allowed for her natural beauty to radiate effortlessly. Her light make-up touches and simple lipstick were ample enough to accomplish the 'night-in' look that she was going for. She took a seat at one of the leather covered Valencia bar stools and listened to Tina. It was becoming more apparent that if Tina took another drink, she'd be ready and willing to be taken advantage of.

Tina placed the wine glass carefully on the countertop and pulled a bottle from the chiller, "I came into this world alone and I will leave it alone," she mumbled while hoisting herself up to sit next to the delicate glass. "Anything else I do in between is solely for my happiness and amusement," she winced. "And you know what? That bitch owes me an apology! I did *her* a favor! I was trying to save her marriage *and* her soul and the dirty whore repays me with a black eye and a busted lip. I couldn't even leave my house for two weeks after that!"

"Humph", Girl X responded as she took a sip from her glass. Tina continued to pout while reaching for a drawer handle attached to the base of the counter. She shuffled a few utensils around before pulling a metal cork screw from its place. Tina grabbed the wine and began the task of opening the bottle. *"Now isn't that the pot calling the kettle black!"* she squeaked. "She had the nerve to chastise me about fighting in a club, but she started a fight in the church house!" *Pop!* The bottle resounded and she picked up the glass awaiting its fill. "The church house!" she said out loud as she filled the glass three fourths of the way full and swung her crossed legs back and forth. From the looks of it, it was clear that Tina had left the church that day with more than a bruised ego. But in her mind, she'd felt like she'd won, like she'd won the

greatest gift of them all, Ray.

Tina took a sip of her wine and began having an audible conversation with herself. "What the hell is wrong with that man?" She took another sip. "He was supposed to see my wounds and nurse me back to health," she said jumping off the countertop. "I gotta admit though, that was a side of Desiree I'd never seen before. Guess I underestimated her," she said with a snicker as she walked over to the gold framed rectangle mirror that rested in the center of the wall behind the bar and leaned in for a closer look. "The girl had a mean punch," she rubbed her face. "I figured she'd get mad, cry a lot, and run out the church. I mean honestly, I only went to church that day to see how the Taylor's would act in front of all the Holy rollers and James didn't disappoint. Although, I really only expected them to request a prayer or three and front like Jesus had really changed anything. *Chile* J.J. gave the performance of a lifetime!" she said turning around to face her companion almost excited. "He turned into a sniveling bitch right there in front of the whole world. *That* in its self made me laugh. But when Desi took the stage I couldn't resist. Something in me wanted to make sure since she was airing her dirty laundry that she aired it all. So I *had* to get up; the power of Christ compelled me," she said taking another sip and checking herself out in the mirror once more, all while Girl X looked on.

"Those old ladies have got strength! *Shit!* Desi was lucky girl, they were holding me back. That's the only thing that saved her hoe ass!"

"The *only* thing?" Girl X asked comically.

"Anyway, at least the church folks did the nice Christian thing and helped me nurse my physical wounds in the basement bathroom. That was the least they could do seeing as I gave them enough gossip to last a life time."

"That much you did do," Girl X said, raising her glass for a rhetorical toast and took a sip.

"I left with an ice pack on my eye. Needless to say it was a hard drive home." Tina giggled at herself. "Once I got here the first phone call I made was to Ray. And do you know he didn't answer. So I left a sweet 'hello baby' message and waited for him to return my call," Tina said concentrating on the liquid in her glass. "He never did," she continued. "I was sure Desi got to him first. I waited for a phone call that would never come," she said somberly and gulped what was left in the glass before pouring another.

"*Girl,* that's a hot ass mess," Girl X finally responded. "I'm not sure what you were expecting from all that drama," she said studying Tina.

"*Tanya*, seriously."

"First, don't use my government name. Second, yes, seriously." Tanya retorted. She liked being known as the no-name mystery woman. It kept life simple in her eyes, however, she'd known Tina for some time and they'd become a lot closer since their first encounter together with Ray. Not to mention, Tina was very attractive and, in some ways, just enough crazy to be interesting.

"Well call it whatever you want. I'm grown and I can make my own decisions. Desi's been too damn perfect for too damn long and somebody had to snatch her ass off that high horse."

"Damn girl, did it have to be you?"

"Who else better to do it than me? I'm her friend. I was helping her out."

"Well, if you ever feel the need to put me in my place, just let me know which palm is fisting the knife first before you stab me in the back," Tanya said seriously.

Tina's laugh was full then halted when she'd noticed Tanya's raised brow. "You have nothing to worry about. We aren't that close."

"You got that right," Tanya said sipping her wine. "Ray was in love with that girl. You were just a party favor for a friend."

Tina paused long enough to process the reality of the situation and quickly denied it. Tanya may have invited her to the party, but she decided to stay.

4
DON'T GET MAD, GET EVEN

When J.J. made *the mistake*, the first and only person he'd told was his best friend, Javán. Whom he'd met in undergrad at a campus mixer and subsequently managed to get arrested together for participating in a fight. That night James was Javán's alibi and Javán was his. Needless to say they got off with a warning. They'd both gone into law and Javán landed a position in the attorney general's office and J.J. landed a sweet position at a private firm.

James told him all the gory details but would not reveal the names of the guilty accomplices. Nevertheless, although Javán was single, he seemed to really understand the life of a married man. It was really Javán who made sure J.J. followed through with the breaking up of the mistake. He actually had to explain to J.J. that he could not be "friends" with a woman who didn't mind sleeping with a married man. As a woman, I personally always appreciated the fact that Javán kept J.J. on track and was never afraid to tell him if he was wrong. Not to mention the fact that he was the most humble of the pair. Which by all accounts made him sexier, but I digress.

J.J.'s colleague Wesley was all together different. There were countless nights when I'd arrive home to see Wes and a new play thing entertaining themselves at my house. I swear I felt like a parent every time he and I crossed paths, warning J.J. about not letting Wes' bad habits rub off on him. Obviously that warning went unheeded. Wesley, on the other hand, was of no assistance when he found out that J.J. had gotten into a scuffle outside of Smith and Wollensky. James still had no idea how the hell Wesley found out. In the days following the bathroom incident, Wes came into James' office with a smug smile and asked how his hand was doing. Wes claimed he'd "heard" through the grapevine that J.J. had an altercation. Knowing Wes knew about the scuffle didn't really matter at that point, so long as no one else found out about his transgressions. James Jones Taylor was not a prideful man, just a private man.

After all is said and done, James is a good guy. Like most people, he doesn't like it when people screw with him, his wife, or his livelihood, but then again who does. It's been my experience that when James feels like someone has crossed him; he doesn't get mad, he gets even. And I mean even in the worst way. He's never been much of the vengeful type until pushed and I think it's fair to say something happened to bring him to the brink of madness. I'd assumed it was because of the whole baby thing but something in the pit of my stomach wouldn't allow me to believe that to be the gospel truth.

Shortly following his encounter with Ray in the bathroom, J.J. returned to the establishment to find out who the scum bag was that claimed he'd fucked his wife. Once J.J. produced two one hundred dollar bills, the valet happily provided the name of the scum bag; none other than Raymond Humphrey. The valet was all too eager to explain that Ray frequents the establishment on a regular basis.

∞ ∞ ∞

James marched into Javán Miller's office and closed the door.

"Hey man. How's it going?" Javán said standing.

"Long time my friend! It's going," J.J. responded with a handshake and a half bodied hug.

"What brings you to the slums of government affairs?" Javán asked patting J.J. on the shoulder.

"Not business, I can assure you of that."

"*Oh,*" Javán said as he took his seat and leaned closer.

"Yeah....It's personal and off the record," J.J. said seriously.

"Agreed," he affirmed. "I'm listening."

"I met this fella in a bathroom a few months back," James started, when he noticed Javán's eyebrow arch. "No. No. No. No. Not like that! Matter of fact, *NOTHING* like that!" With his hand over his chest, Javán took a deep sigh of relief and relaxed. "I want you to look into someone for me. I need to know everything there is to possibly know about this guy," James continued.

"Should I even ask why?" he asked rhetorically.

"You know better than to ask questions that you already know the answer to."

"Enough said. I have a feeling the less I know the better!" he laughed. "So what's the name of the unknown suspect?"

5
STOP THE WORLD I WANT TO GET OFF

"Desiree Elizabeth Taylor!" The buzzer went on *buzz buzz buzz*. "If you don't open this door I'm gonna open it for you!" *buzz buzz buzz buuuuuzzzzzzzzzzzz*. Finally it stopped. I was hoping Tara would go away. I just wasn't in the mood for cheering up or girl talk. I just wanted to lie in my bed and watch the silent movie going on inside my head. It was a fascinating movie too. Well, to be honest, it was really just a replay of my life and every time I play it over I change the ending. So far none of what I've come up with has been to my liking. Apparently I lack the imagination it takes to change my very own life in my own head. Just as I was about to start my movie over, I felt a gush of something wet hit me in the face. I squeezed my eyes and gasped.

"What the hell!" I said struggling to my feet trying to focus my eyes.

"Get up! I'm sick of this!" Tara said in the most firm tone I'd ever heard come out of her mouth. "I've been calling and calling and calling. You've got everybody worried sick about you and you have the nerve to not even acknowledge I was at your door," she said as she walked around my bed and opened either side of my blackout curtains. The light shining through the window was blinding.

"How did you get in here?!" I questioned, still trying to gather my thoughts.

"You gave me an emergency key," she said holding it in the air. "Remember?"

"*Oh.* Well, this isn't an emergency so now you've officially abused your key powers."

"It *is* an emergency when you don't answer my calls for two weeks and you take off from work and hide in this place. I didn't know if you were in here rotting to death or not. And from the looks of it you may not be dead but you look like death warmed over."

"Hey! Watch it! I take a shower daily."

"I didn't say you smelled rotten."

"Then why did you dump water on me?"

"Honestly, it just made me happy. You made me worry, so I made you wet," she said in a *nah-nah* kind of tone.

"Now you don't have to be worried. You see me. I'm fine."

"No, you're not fine. You are alive and breathing but you're not fine," Tara stood facing me with that twisted look of concern in her eyes. She was almost crying. "I think it's time." She said standing in front of me and placing her hands on my shoulders. "It's time for you to see someone about what's troubling you. You can't hide away from the world."

"I'm not," I lied. "I just needed a break from life so I took one. There is nothing wrong with that," I said moving away from her gaze.

"Yes there is. If you haven't found a solution,

what good is it doing you to lock yourself away?"

"Lots, Tara! I've got to figure this out on my own."

"Desi, no one is trying to figure it out for you. Sometimes you just need to say it out loud to someone who you know is listening and has nothing to do with the any of it."

"Yeah but --"

"No buts! You are going and you're insurance will pay for it 'cause I've already had you declared legally insane," she giggled and glanced out the window.

"What are you looking at?" I asked curiously. "Who's out there?"

"Nobody," she said quickly.

"Nope! You're lying. Who is that?" I said moving toward the window.

"Okay. Okay," she said stepping in front of me to block my view. "You really had me worried so I came right over."

"*Who is outside Tara?!*"

"Nobody you'd know. I had a date and I asked him to swing by here first."

"You brought your date to my house. What the hell is wrong with you girl! I'm fine. Now get your behind back in that car. Why are you making him wait? That's why you're single," I went on. "Get out of my house and leave the key. Bye!"

"Desi, you would know I've been seeing someone for the last few weeks if you'd answer the phone. So shut up and get away from the window," she said pulling me away from the curtain. "He's already learning how to deal with me and you gave him a college education on how important my friends are in my life."

"So you've talked about my business with a stranger!"

"No. Don't be stupid. I just told him I had to do a wellness check on an insane person."

"*Real funny T!*"

"Not at all."

"So where did you meet this exceptional stranger?" I asked coyly.

"In St. Thomas, when I went to visit my mother." Tara darted her eyes at me, "Don't you say a word!"

"I'm not. I'm just listening. You may continue," I said with a sly smile.

"*Anyway!* I took one of those boat tours to the island and he happened to be the captain and owner of the fleet."

"So you brought him home?"

"Uh, no! Geez girl, let me finish," Tara said in a slightly annoyed tone. "He is actually from here and spends time in both places so he is here for awhile and I decided to accept his invitation to get to know each other a little bit while he's in town. Is that okay with you?"

"Nope! Not until I meet him."

"You will, just not today you mental case."

"Shut up. I'm not a mental case, insane, crazy, or even delusional. I'm just on a break from life. We've been over this already."

Tara rolled her eyes, "Like I said, not today."

"Okay fine. Be that way," I said turning on my heels and walking into the kitchen.

"What are you up to Desiree Elizabeth?!" Tara said walking behind me.

"Nothing. You said not today, so okay."

"I know you too well for this Desi."

"You didn't say tomorrow. So...I'm sure between now and then your moms will fill me in and I will be all caught up by the time we have dinner TOMORROW night."

"Oh *hell* no! Absolutely not!"

"You said you wanted me up and back in the land of the living so here I am and you just gave me the best reason of all," I said pinching her cheeks.

"And what would that be?" she asked smacking my hand away from her face and leaning against the counter. I noticed she was standing the way she always did when she was preparing for an argument, palms backwards and flat against the counter's edge as if she was ready to push off at any given moment.

"You're love life silly! Fixing you, in that area at least, has been my greatest challenge," I shrugged. "You just gave me something to focus on besides my own disastrous life. You've got a better chance at matters of the heart because I am a walking, living, breathing guide on what not to do."

"Oh my gosh Desi, no you're not and I don't need fixing, that's you!"

"Didn't I just admit that! Dang you don't listen at all. Some friend you are."

"Whatever. Call this lady TODAY! Go lay on her couch! I have to go, I have a date," she said placing the card on my table and closed the door.

"I love to hate you!" I yelled after her. That's

when I noticed the smile I didn't realize had
appeared on my face was still there. Great friends
are hard to find! Hell, I should know.
In my lifetime I've heard of people seeing a
therapist for extreme situations or emotional trauma
but I didn't consider myself or the situation to fit in
either of those categories. That was until...I saw
Raymond in a shopping center one day with a
young woman. I hid behind a rack of panties in the
lingerie section until they passed. I quickly click
clacked my way to the exit then to my car where,
once inside, I promptly began hyperventilating. This
happened on more than one occasion even with
Raymond look-a-likes. That's when I knew this was
"that" category.

6
WHAM, BAM, THANK YOU MA'AM

Ray awoke this particular morning with his typical morning wood. He lay underneath the Egyptian cotton sheets, eyes half open, until he heard the sound of his alarm resounding throughout the house. He flipped the sheets backwards and threw is legs over the side of the bed. Before standing up, he glanced at his naked lower half and admired himself. His package was impressive even to himself. Once his feet were firmly planted on the freshly waxed hardwood floors he bypassed the alarm and went into the bathroom to wash his face and brush his teeth. He decided to go downstairs where he picked up the remote resting on the top of the couch. He flipped on the television and scrolled the channels for Sports Center, then tossed the remote on the seat cushion and made his way into the adjacent kitchen where he turned on the coffee pot and picked up a half eaten donut from an open box that was beginning to go stale. He poured a hot cup of coffee and remembered his current state. Limp dicks and hot coffee don't really pair well so he took a seat at the kitchen table.

"Sometimes things and people we leave behind in life often come back to haunt us every

once in awhile. My house hasn't been the same since Desiree was here." That's what was on Raymond's mind this morning as he held the cup of coffee, sitting at the kitchen table staring out the window. He'd drowned out the background noise from the radio and television, everything became quiet, but then again it's always quiet. Ray's mind trailed as he imagined the backyard with a child enjoying the morning playing. He couldn't shake the feeling that somehow it felt different the day I arrived, he felt whole and so did his house. His house was officially home. As a man, Ray felt as though he couldn't risk showing me that – he'd have too much to lose and he did. He lost in his mind. He rationalized those situations like ours was the reason why he didn't share his heart or his space with anyone. He was broken – even defeated. There was so much Ray could have said or done to change the outcome but.... *"Man up!"* Raymond said out loud as he sat up straight, stuck out his chest, then like a sail that's lost its wind; he slumped back down and stared into his coffee cup as if it was a magic eight ball. He started reminiscing on the many nights we'd had with each other. One in particular came to mind.

"So you love me?" Desiree asked.

"Who wouldn't? I would be a fool not to," Ray said without hesitation.

"That's the first time you've ever said that to me." As the declaration swayed from Ray's lips to Desiree's ears, her already wide eyes grew and her gaze at Ray intensified.

Ray sat paralyzed at the realization, *"Well..."*

was all he could say.

"Why?" She asked sheepishly.

"Don't ask any more questions," Ray said turning away.

That night Ray made long passionate love to a woman he'd actually loved; me. He made me climax at least three times. The entire night he took it low and slow, even when I begged him to 'go harder' or fuck me, he went slow. Purposefully slow. Ray wanted every inch of me to feel every inch of him. He determined making love to me in this way was the best, easiest and most effective way he could truly show me that he'd meant what he said. "I love you." He let those three words slip past his lips as he felt his dick harden again. "Butt naked at the kitchen table with a woody, what a way to start the morning," Ray shook his head.

Ray placed the cup of coffee, now cold, on the table and headed to the bathroom to take a shower. He opened the glass door, turned the knob to hot and promptly stepped in. The mixture of immediate cold then hot kept his member at attention. He reached for the bar of soap resting on the steal shower caddy. He lathered both hand and began massaging his third leg as he moaned the name "Desiree" while he ferociously stroked himself until an explosion of white creamy liquid forced its way out onto the shower floor and down the drain.

∞ ∞ ∞

"Just when I think I finally shook it off! It's nothing short of some kind of crazy sign." Ray said shaking as he paced the floor. He couldn't believe it,

34

"Out of all the people to run into today!"

"Man what's wrong with you?" Wesley questioned.

"Nothing," Ray said looking at his hands tremble. "That's the problem. I'm fine. I'm really okay."

"Okay Ray, I think you need to really sit down."

"No. No I don't. I need to get myself together and figure this out," Ray responded still looking at his hands.

"Figure what out? I'm confused. What happened?"

Ray stopped pacing and turned his head to face the only other person in the room; Wesley. His face read like a suspense thriller at its climax. Ray cleared his throat before he began to speak. "I was at the gas station this morning getting some coffee. I went to pay for my gas and coffee but I had this weird feeling that someone was watching me but I didn't see anybody. It was just weird. I don't normally get freaked out about stuff like that but I don't know. Anyway, you remember I told you there was this female that had my nose open awhile ago?"

"Yeah, so," Wes responded.

"Well, I was pulling out of the gas station onto ninth and this car was passing. I guess I was still trying to figure out if someone was following me and I hit this car going by."

"Was anybody hurt? You didn't kill anyone did you?"

"Nah, everybody was fine," Ray assured

him.

"So what does this have to do with that female?" Wesley asked curiously.

"It was her! That's who I hit! I side swiped her car coming out the gas station," Ray shouted frantically.

"What?!" Wes said as he eased to the front of his seat.

"Yes! I didn't know it was her until I got out and checked on the car."

"What did she say?"

"I was so stunned....almost happy to see her. She was shaken up of course but when she saw my face she just sat there staring."

"So she *was* hurt?"

"No. She wasn't hurt or at least that's how it turned out. I thought she was so I opened her door and helped her out of the car. I inspected her from head to toe and apologized profusely. She finally just said she was fine and looked at the damage to her car. So I told her to give me her info so I could get it all fixed up and she wouldn't. I tried assuring her that it was strictly for insurance purposes only and by that time the police pulled up and they separated us and handled it."

"So that was it?"

"Yeah....She could barely look at me," Ray recalled the scene in his head.

"You said it ended badly, right? So what else did you want her to say?"

"I don't know. The whole scene was awkward. She got her police report and left. She acted like she didn't even know me."

"I'm sure it was better that way."

"I'm not. I have her info now and ever since this morning I'm still trembling and still thinking about her," Ray held his hands out and watched them. His nerves had gotten the better of him.

"It was a near death experience that's all. You'll be fine," Wes said with a wave of his hand.

"Yeah, I'm sure you're right. One of those life flashes before your eyes moments."

"Yep!"

"Maybe I should call my mother," Ray laughed.

"Maybe you should call on Jesus," Wesley said as he stood.

"Ain't *no* helping me bruh. Now get out. I got work to do."

"Alright. Can I get you some coffee before I go?" Wesley said jokingly.

"Get out!" Ray said with a deep laugh. He paused and shook his head at the vision of that woman. It was hard to concentrate from that point forward.

7
FOR BETTER OR WORSE

Cheating on me was unthinkable once upon a time. To this day I still can't figure out what possessed James to do so. We busted Pandora's Box wide open when all the secrets, sex, and decadence came tumbling out.

James sat in his office reviewing a folder delivered by messenger a little over an hour before. It was thick and filled with pictures, documents, and other personal identifying information. He combed through the pages highlighting items that peaked his interest. He picked up the passport photo of Raymond and stared at it intently. He glared at the photo and whispered, "Why did she do this to me? We've been through so much and all I want her to do is come home." The thought of me with another man almost crippled our relationship but somehow J.J. was choosing to forgive me, although I still stand by the fact that none of this would have happened if he hadn't done it first.

"What else can I do? I fucked up but she can't keep holding this over my head," he said absent mindedly as he picked up the phone and dialed.

"Hello," my purposefully perky voice

answered the line.

"Oh! Hi. Um..." James answered surprised.

"Hi." I said sweetly.

"Uh, I...um....How are you?" James said searching for words.

"Fine. How are you?"

"Doing well, thanks for asking." He cleared his throat and continued, "So Mrs. Taylor what have you been up to?"

"Nothing and everything at the same time. This task of getting myself in order is nothing short of hopeless," I said with a sigh. "Bet you didn't know it took a village and a shrink to raise me," I said giggling at my own joke.

"Yeah, well I figured it took something greater than me."

"*Humph!* So what you tryna say?!"

"Nothing," he laughed. "Just agreeing with you." The smile widened on his face. It felt good to laugh again.

"Nice save Mr. Taylor."

"Hey it's what I do."

"I'm so sure."

"So, I was wondering if we could meet for lunch or dinner or something?"

"Um...I'm not sure if that's a good idea," my hesitation alarmed him.

"Why not?"

"Because I'm a hot mess right now and --"

"Listen, we've seen each other at our worst and I still love you. If I can't be there for you when you're a hot mess then what purpose do I serve in your life?" James said with sincere authority.

"I know...it's complicated," I admitted. Thoughts of Ray still lingered in the back of my mind.

"Nothing can be more complicated than what we've already been through."

I paused to think about it for a moment, and then answered, "Ok. How about lunch?"

"Ok great! How about tomorrow at Debbie's Soul Food?"

"Ok. See you then, around noon-ish."

"It's a date!" he said excited.

"No, it's lunch," I said quickly before hanging up. J.J. looked at the phone and placed it on the receiver. My last statement made him feel cold. He shrugged it off and decided to smile at the thought of seeing his wife again.

∞ ∞ ∞

When I'd walked into the restaurant, he stood to greet me and I hardly allowed him to hug me. Seeing him standing there made me feel like a Jezebel. He pulled out my chair and I politely accepted the seat across from his. When he sat down he looked me in my eyes. They were filled with a mixture of coldness and tears. There was obviously an internal battle taking place and I hadn't decided which emotion was going to win. Seeing James be the gentleman I once knew softened me just enough to remember why I'd loved him in the first place. As we spoke, I couldn't shake the nauseating image of his lips on another woman.

Lunch was a variation of awkward silences,

reminiscing, and endearing looks from across the table. *"She was different. There was something about her that was definitely different. Not physically but...there was a vibe very unfamiliar to me,"* he thought. That gut reaction made him change his plan and the tone of the lunch. All he'd wanted to do was hug me, kiss me, and hold me in his arms but the uncertain feeling in the air instantly changed all of that. We both tried to feel the other out until he finally asked, "So what's it going to take to get you home?"

Without looking in his eyes I responded, "I don't know." When I gained enough courage to look at him again, the look of pain on his face was like nothing I'd ever seen before.

"I'm still here. I love you. I need you. I want you."

"Thank you for saying that. All of this has changed me J.J. Honestly, I don't know if I'm still the woman you think you love. I don't even know myself anymore," I said sitting back fidgeting with my necklace.

"I'm not the same man either. In a lot of ways I've changed too." He took a deep breath. "All I can say is we agreed that we are Mister and Misses Taylor for better or worse."

Those words struck me to my very core. I've been struggling with that very thing for far too long. *Does all the stuff we've done to each other negate those words? Were they just words?* They always meant something to me until something that forced them into play happened. I want happily ever after. I *really* do but I want mine with a side of spice.

Maybe that's too much to ask. I withdrew my hand
from his and went back to fidgeting with my
necklace.

∞ ∞ ∞

The morning after my lunch with James I
was calm, cool, and collected as I lay on my side
surrounded by nine pillows staked around my head,
snuggled under the oversized duvet comforter. The
sheets felt baby soft against my skin as my head
rested on my hands. I was finally calm again. My
session with Dr. Anirbas actually had a side effect;
calmness. The confusion over my situation was
starting to dissipate.

I got up to unpack more boxes. I needed this
place to feel like home, even if it was temporary.
The bedroom was the perfect place to start, no need
to venture out any further. Baby steps right? One
thing at a time, as I went through each box and
placed items where I thought they should go. When
I got to the box holding my jewelry, I made sure to
set the crystal ring box that held my wedding ring
on top. It was my feature, my reminder that
someone still loved me and I need to do what's right
for the both of us, whatever right may turn out to
be.

I knew my day of reckoning would come
soon but I had no idea it would come so fast and
furiously.

8

THE QUIET BEFORE THE STORM

I walked into the brown brick building and straight into the office and closed the door. The waiting room consisted of a few strategically placed plants, a brown cloth couch, two brown leather chairs on either side of the couch and a glass coffee table in the center. The receptionist desk was tall with a privacy nook covering most of it, next to a single door. Very simple in motif, which kind of made sense if you thought about it, people come to places like this to find simplicity. Everything served a purpose.

"Good morning Mrs. Taylor. How can I help you?" the cheerful receptionist greeted me.

"Good morning. I have the first AM appointment."

"Yes, I've got it right here. No need to wait go ahead and go in."

"Thank you Nancy. By the way you're glowing," I said with a wink and a smile. I strutted my way toward the door and exhaled once it closed behind me. My mind and body were drained. I hadn't slept in three days and I'd just used that last ounce of energy on that rented smile. My shoulders slumped and entered the second door on the right.

"I'm tired." I said entering the room without so much as a *hello* and closed the door behind me.

"Nice to see you, Desiree," the woman behind the desk said looking up.

"I'm tired," I said sitting down on the couch closest to the door. "It's nice to see you too."

"I see you're ready to jump in today."

"Yep! You can tell huh?"

"Well," she said moving to the seat adjacent to mine. "Let's dig right in then. The last time you were here we made a lot of progress. And for the first time, you started to talk about your family and childhood. Should we start there?"

"No, that's what's got me drained. Let's start with the week I've had so far."

"Okay. I'm listening."

"I'm feeling better about the way things are going and I'm beginning to see that this separation from J.J. was a good choice. I've had to do a lot of soul searching and decision-making lately and I feel really good about it."

"Go on," she encouraged.

"After I left here last week I met J.J. for lunch and asked him to give me some quiet space for awhile. He was agreeable. I told him about our session and how you'd help me uncover some things in my past that I needed to deal with alone. He said that he understood and told me he'd be patient."

"Were you surprised by his response?"

"I'm not really sure. At that moment I don't think it mattered. What mattered was me being able to tell him that. For me it was more about the communication."

"Why was that important?"

"Because we've been through hell and back and I wanted him to know that this is where I am at. I know he loves me...*is* still in love with me and he deserves that much," I said sweetly.

"That must feel good, to know someone loves you."

"It does," I replied. "He's been extremely comforting...to know both of us are going through counseling independently before we try it together."

"It's been a little while since the incident. Do you think about it?" she asked seriously.

"Every day and every other day. I can't help but think what my child would be like. What would it have felt like to be a mother....To have a family?" My eyes began to water. "And the fact that I will never know now. I can never give my husband a child. That hurts the most and I have no one to blame but myself."

"Do you think he would've been happy raising another man's child?"

"No. I don't know how that would've worked out for either of us...them...everyone involved. I'd like to think I would've been able to handle it better but I think we both know the answer to that," I said with a sigh.

"I think it's time to address a major player in all this."

"Who? Ray? Nope. No way. Too soon. Not ready."

"I can see that. I'm referring to Tina. You've hardly mentioned her since we've started these sessions."

"That's because she doesn't exist to me anymore."

9
THREE WORDS

"I miss you. I love you."

That's how it all started. The significance of three little words held the weight of the world. His stomach was in knots when he said them. Before he could put his tail between his legs and run Raymond let the words gallivant out of my mouth as he stood there on an oddly chilly September night. He watched as the mist of frosty air carried them from his lips to my ears.

Ray stood frozen as he stared at the back of my coat walking away from him. Then for a brief moment he prayed that I hadn't heard the words he'd never allowed anyone to hear him say. I stopped. In what felt like the longest breath a person could take I didn't turn around before I spoke. "Don't."

Ray said nothing. His mind told him to leave but his body wouldn't move.

"I...miss you too," I said softly.

He managed to exhale upon hearing those words struggle from my mouth. With that I continued a hurried walk to the parking garage and disappeared around the corner of the entrance. He stood there silently smiling at himself for allowing himself to say something this time.

Raymond decided to bite the bullet and contacted his insurance company for my contact information. Upon receiving my cell phone number, he promptly sent a message requesting that I call him when I got a chance. He made sure to explain it was urgent. I instantly became nervous but chose to find out what was so urgent that he couldn't tell me when he saw me. Later that evening, the rain fell hard as I ended my phone call and pulled into a parking space of the forest preserve, next to a champagne colored BMW i3 with black tinted windows. I took a deep breath and unlocked the doors of my SUV and patiently waited.

The car door of the BMW opened slowly and an umbrella popped up before Ray stood up to exit the vehicle. He wasn't wearing a jacket and he was holding a bouquet of roses. His arms flexed in the black dress shirt and his height seemed more pronounced in his black dress slacks. He closed the door and quickly opened mine and hopped in. He collapsed his umbrella and shook it a little before he set it on the floor of the car. Without hesitation he handed the flowers to me and leaned over the center console and kissed my cheek before speaking. I noticed the small black and red card nestled between them. I thanked him with a smile and set them on the backseat.

"I'm so glad to see you," Ray said sincerely.

"I'm glad you contacted me."

"Before this goes any further, I would really like for Desi to be here, not Desiree. We are not in the boardroom."

"Oookay," I said with a roll of my eyes.

"Seriously, Desi. Nothing is going to get resolved if you come at me in that cut throat manner you are famous for."

I thought about his request for a moment and adjusted my demeanor. "Fair enough."

"Ok. Good. How are you?"

"I'm doing fine, just making some adjustments here and there. How are you?"

"The same," he paused and swallowed hard. "I need you to know that I love you first and foremost. I also need you know that I'm so sorry for all of the drama. That wasn't something I ever intended for either of us to go through." He looked down at his hands then back into my eyes. "Honestly I don't know where we went wrong...but what I do know is that you are the best thing to ever happen to me and I need you in my life."

I sat still for a moment to digest his words before responding. "Fuck you," I said calmly. My eyes felt as though they penetrated his soul when I said it.

"What?!" he said surprised.

"Fuck you," I repeated.

"What the hell is wrong with you?! I just sat here and poured my heart out to you with a sincere apology and this is how you respond!"

"You have no idea how long I've been waiting to say that," I said with a sigh of relief. "You asked for Desi and you got her," I reminded him.

"I know things...they didn't turn out right and again I'm so sorry."

"I honestly don't care about your sorry. You left me alone, vulnerable and scared," I said with a snarl.

"Why don't we call it a night?"

"Yeah, I think that's a good idea."

"*Oookay*..." Ray said trying to not sound disappointed at the acceptance of his own suggestion. "I agree that there is a lot we need to talk about, calmly, so when can we do that? No lust involved, I promise."

The next thing I knew, the fogged ridden windows of my car reminded me of a time when I would have make out sessions like this one with J.J. except this time it wasn't him, it was Ray. I had no idea our "talk" would turn into an hour long groping session. It started with pleasantries, turned into an argument, and that somehow converted into Ray touching my leg with his tongue down my throat and his hands twisting my nipples like radio knobs. I have no clue how my hand ended up planted firmly around the thickness of his exposed shaft while my thumb rotated around the head. At my reluctant instance we paused to take breather. I was panting and fanning myself like the southern bell I'm clearly not.

"Okay, this is getting too hot."

"Not hot enough if you ask me," Ray said with a big smile.

"How did we end up like this?" I said looking at his still very erect penis.

"Don't question it. You know how we feel about each other. The chemistry between us is ridiculous."

"That may be true but there is so much more wrong with this; with you and I, which this shouldn't even be happening."

"Wrong?"

"You know what I mean Ray," I said with a sneer.

"That's the past. Why can't we leave it there?" he asked almost sad.

"Because it's all unresolved, that's why."

"Do we have to talk about it now? Can't we just have this moment? I've missed you so much," he pleaded.

"No Ray, we can't. This is what is destroying me...."

"Destroying you?" he said sitting up confused.

"Yes. All of this..." I said waving my hands over his body,"has got me in therapy."

"Damn! I didn't know I got to you like that Desi."

"All of it did. I'm trying to put the pieces back together and doing what we are doing is never ever going to help that."

Ray thought for a moment and began to pull himself together. "You are right."

"We finally agree on something," I said sarcastically.

"Listen, I want you in the worst way...in every way but I also want you in the right way."

"Who says you can have me?"

"You did. Just now," he answered quickly. "With your actions. With your words. You never said I couldn't."

"Aren't you cute," I responded pinching his cheeks like a child. "I'm not yours for the taking."

"That's what you say now."

"Plus, I've got something very important I need to work out and tell you," I confessed.

"You can tell me anything."

"Not anything."

"Okay fine, everything."

"Give me a couple of days. I need to clear my head," I said staring out the windshield.

"I can do that. But I want you to know something D....I love you more than you'll ever understand. It's not just sex."

"I don't know how to respond to that Ray."

"And *I* don't know how to respond to that," he said defensively then quickly changed his tone. "Never mind, no need to."

"Don't start." I shot back.

"No, I'm not starting anything. I going to get out of this car and make my way home. Then take a cold shower and remind myself that you are worth the wait."

My immediate eye roll at the utterance of those words made it clear to him that he had gone too far. "I'm going. I'm going," he quickly recovered. With a hand placed lightly on my face he gave me a peck on the cheek and exited my vehicle. I couldn't help but smile at the sweetness of the sentiment. I drove away before he'd closed the door of his own car.

10
CRAZY

Inside the small black and red card left inside the bouquet of roses, was a handwritten invitation from Ray to be his guest at a local gala fundraiser. The cause was domestic violence and he knew it held a soft spot in my heart. I thought about going and then not going over and over again, until finally I made a decision. Everybody plays the fool right? Well, I've got a second chance at this thing and I wasn't going to screw it up.

In Ray's mind, all he had to do is show me that he was the man I wanted; the man I needed. Ray elected to play his hand one more time. He felt as though he had a few trumps in his hand. For example, James never gave me a baby, a threesome or anal sex. If he'd learned anything in his life it was that most women couldn't resist a great lover. It didn't matter what they did, all they had to do is lay the pipe and you'd forget about being mad or disappointed. Ray should have an Olympic medal for all the games he played and won. But he knew this was going to take an extra special effort. The stakes were higher and the prize was too great. Ray could be an asshole pure and simple but I considered it a part of his charm versus a character flaw.

Ray's hands shook on the steering wheel as he waited in his car. He couldn't help it. His nerves were too bad. He contemplated smoking but quickly remembered that he didn't smoke. He waited in that car for hours hoping I'd accepted his invitation. He watched the front door of the hotel like a hawk! Once I arrived, he planned to walk in after me so as not to appear too eager. He reached down to turn the station on the radio. Ray knew after our encounter that he would have to work fast to get me to even consider entertaining him again. He told me once that his mother used to tell him that love is passion; people forget their heads and listen to their impulses, no matter how irrational. And this couldn't be more irrational for him.

I pulled in front of the hotel and allowed the valet to whisk my chariot away. My hair was swept up in a tight bun with a feathered bang draped to one side. My red and white diamond tear drop earrings with matching bracelet sparkled from my limbs. I wore a floor length long white satin gown that adorned every curve in just the right places. The shoulder straps were wide over the curve of my shoulders but the design made my sweetheart bust line pronounced. My red heels and clutch made for the perfect pop off color. I appreciated the dress and my hair for their simplicities and complexities, just like I'd pictured my evening. I looked down and pinched the front of my dress to pull it up so as not to stumble and gingerly stepped into the lobby. The room was filled with people, some whom I knew and others who I'd never met but always wanted the pleasure of meeting.

The concierge escorted me on the private elevator to the top floor where the first thing I laid eyes on was an immaculate view of the entire city. The city lights sparkled in my eyes and danced with me for a few moments. I entered the ballroom and stood in amazement. The purple up-lighting and gold down-lighting reflected off of the white tablecloths with gold accents like water reflects the sun. There was a big band on the stage playing a nice jazz melody that somehow morphed into a well-known R & B ballot. Just like the tables, the stage was lined with alternating bouquets of purple flowers and white orchids sprayed with a glistening gold dust. The wooden dance floor was open in the center of the room. Events like these never ceased to amaze me. They were special in their own way and being there made me feel special in my own way.

I was having a lovely conversation with the executive director of one of the featured organizations when Ray walked up behind me.

"Will you excuse me for a moment?" I said with a smile to the organization's director. She politely excused herself but not before she gave me a sly smile with a wink.

"You look beautiful," Ray said in the deepest voice he could muster.

"Looks like a hell-of-a party," I replied without acknowledging his compliment.

"Every man in this room is wondering who you're here with. I had to come over to put their minds at ease. Plus this gives me a chance to observe the competition," he said still standing behind me close enough that I could feel his breath on my neck. The tiny hairs on my neck stood at attention as I placed my palm over the area.

"Where did that come from?" I asked turning to face my ex-lover. "Is this a form of stalking? Am I in danger?" I said as he kissed my neck. "I don't know what to think."

"If anything ever happened to you I *swear* I wouldn't be able to live," Ray declared.

"Ok I just got here and you're already scaring me," I said looking around the room as I lifted a glass of wine from the waiter passing by. "I don't know what to think Mr. Humphrey."

"Think I'm crazy in love. Think I'm handsome. Think...nothing," he said staring into my eyes with such great intensity my body shook with chills. "Truth be told, I'm not crazy Desiree. I'm just --"

"Crazy!" I said with certainty.

"You've been on my mind," Ray whispered. "I'm sorry it took me so long to come to my senses."

"Honestly, I don't know why I'm here," I said looking away from the intensity in his eyes. "I have so much to figure out. There are real things we need to discuss and going on a date to a gala is probably not the best way to start that conversation."

"What happened to you?" he asked serious and concerned.

"*Me?*"

"Yes, you. Where is my Desi. I know she's in there hiding just dying to come out and play."

"No. Desi, I mean Desiree is standing right

here and I haven't gone anywhere. I'm trying to behave myself like a lady should. And you...you are trying to send me to a grave of ecstasy. That, I might add, I did not ask for."

He moved in front of me, his tall frame casting a half shadow across my body. He looked down into my round face and held his gaze until I silently begged him to stop. The moisture between my thighs increased in flow and intensity. He kissed my cheek ever so gently and whispered in my ear, "You are here because this is the start over that both of us wanted. It's the first step in my plan to prove to you that I am worthy. There will be plenty of time for discussion. Tonight is just about being friends in a public place without avoiding one another." He took my glass from my hands and took a sip before continuing. "There is a fine line between ecstasy and crazy and I like living on the edge," he said pulling away. I couldn't speak. I knew he was right; I liked the edge too. He turned and walked away. This was just like him to turn foolishness into something sexy. Although I couldn't blame him, sex was the one area where we were most compatible in every way.

I followed after him like a lost puppy who'd found its master. He pulled a chair from the table to allow me to sit. I took the seat and the program began. Just as the lights dimmed, Ray took my hand and held it underneath the table. I looked around the room to see if anyone noticed but no one even looked our direction. I felt myself blush as he squeezed my hand tighter.

That night, I left the gala with the warmest

feeling I've felt in months. A simple hug was all it took to send me on my way. I was happy that it had gone so well.

∞ ∞ ∞

Ray grabbed the hooked-tipped black vibrator and asked me to relax. "Don't tense. Just allow yourself to feel."

It took a moment for me to respond because I was trying to fully process what he was asking me to do. After a few moments, I laid down on my back on the floor, spread my legs Indian style, and focused on the ceiling fan. Our outbursts of lustful fits were not new, however, they were pushed into the area of our brains marked, *DO NOT OPEN*. All of this was very new to us again. He could tell that I was hesitant...almost scared. He didn't seem to care about the patch pattern of thorns woven about my lower abdomen but I did. I felt ugly....ashamed. My eyes wondered away from his as if I were searching for an escape or any reason to not do what we were about to do. Before Ray could change my mind, he turned the speed of the vibrator to low, spread the lips of my plumpness with two fingers, and placed it at the opening. He opted not to go in. Instead he just traced the folds of my rose slowly.

"Close your eyes," Ray directed. I did as he'd asked. "Focus on the feeling. When it gets intense relax even more. I'm not going anywhere," he reminded me as he continued tracing my outline. Unexpectedly, I started to moan in an understated tone and Ray paused just enough to let the sensation settle. The tip of his tongue found the ball of my clit. As he licked it I counted the seconds up and the seconds down, five each way to be exact. He could feel the oval in my center pulsate in his mouth, then sat back to watch the involuntary twitching with his own eyes. I didn't open my eyes but I did stretch my arms out and attempted to grab handfuls of the carpet. Ray's eyes watched my body in amazement. To Ray, I was every bit as voluptuous and angelic as a woman could get. And for the time being I was all his, albeit temporary.

He wanted me to remember him in the most endearing way. He watched as the feelings of love and lust returned to my physical body. That's when he reached up to caress my face. "I've missed you like crazy," he whispered. "In my mind, body and soul I kept telling myself that I'm not in love with you," he continued, now hovered over my body. "I finally stopped lying to myself Desiree," Ray's eyes were aflame with sincerity.

"I'm not trying to get hurt again Ray," I finally responded.

"Me either," he said lowering his body on top of mine. Our eyes were locked. Ray searched mine for a silent "no" or "stop" but didn't see any inkling of either of those responses.   He placed a condom over the mound that was him and slid into me with ease. An eye roll of ecstasy came across his face before kissing me. It felt so right, we were so connected. I wrapped my arms underneath his armpits and my fingers pressed into his back pushing his body closer to mine. He didn't stroke or move in and out of me. Ray just allowed his member to take its rightful place inside its rightful owner. We kissed and kissed and kissed and kissed. His package didn't lose its girth. Being kissed like this had the same effect on me as well. The walls of her tunnel started to contract around his dick causing him to explode inside of me. We lay next to each other and just stared at one another. No words came to either of us. But I'm glad they didn't, there were none that needed to be spoken. I placed my head on his chest and we slept.

The sun crept its way through the silk curtains and Ray lay perfectly still so as not to disturb my slumber. I was sleeping so soundly that he didn't want to wake me. As I began to stir, he rubbed my back and arms.

"Good morning beautiful," he said kissing me on the forehead.

"Good morning," I said looking up at him.

"How did you sleep?"

"Fine. How about you?" I asked.

"Like a baby," Ray said with a smile. He noticed that I looked away; my eyes quickly went from sparkling to sadness. "Poor choice of words. I'm sorry," he said sincerely.

"It's ok Ray," I said somberly.

"We can try again, I'm sure we'll be successful. Humphrey men have strong swimmers," he said with a chuckle.

"I think I should be getting home," I said quickly. "Thank you for a wonderful evening."

When I arrived home I tossed my shoes to the side, flopped on my couch, and drifted off to sleep still smiling.

11
SET UPS ARE EASY

Wesley took the afternoon off to run a few errands and tie up some lose ends. He drove up and down the red brick boulevard looking for a familiar face, when he spotted *the mistake* sitting at the window of a bakery shop. He parked his car in the diagonal space in front of the establishment and pressed his horn twice. She looked up from her book and proceeded to join him on the passenger side of the car.

"Well hello there!" she said seductively.

"Hello," Wes responded. "Time has been good to you," he flirted.

"When has it ever been bad?"

"Good point," Wes said leaning against his door.

"Does this little meeting mean you're ready?"

"No. Not yet. I just wanted to see you."

"Should I feel special?" she quipped.

"Yes you should, actually," he said seriously.

She turned her head to look him in the eye as she felt a tinge of annoyance roll over her like a wave of heat. "Don't ever flatter yourself that much Wesley. This isn't, nor will it ever be that!"

"Wooh wooh wooh calm down little lady.

Put the claws back in their place. I was actually thinking that you're my type of woman."

"I'm no one's type. It's just acting with a few perks," she said seriously.

"Call it what you want but your damn good at it."

"Thanks. Now what am I really here for? There are no refunds."

Wes laughed deep and patted her leg. He really thought what she did for him was a turn-on and the fact that she was so very direct about it was amazing in itself. "Nah, I would never ask for a refund on services already rendered."

"So get to it. I've got things I need to do today. My business doesn't run itself."

"I've always wondered how women like yourself end up providing such services."

"You mean to men like you? Yeah it's pretty simple. Your type wants it and my type has it. I just have the balls to make money off of it. Everybody wins."

"Fair enough," Wes said scanning her body. "Too bad you're sloppy seconds. We could have had a future together."

"Listen!" *the mistake* snapped. "We have a business arrangement counselor. If anything other than that has crossed your rabbit ass mind, think again. The next time I want to hear from you is when it's time to close out our deal. Final payment is due 24 hours before," she said getting out of the car but before she could slam the door Wes shouted, "Lady K.? More like Madame!"

"Go fuck yourself!" Lady K. said through

clinched jaws slamming the door.

"Well that went south quickly," Wes said pulling out of the parking space.

As Wesley drove away he couldn't help but smile at his uncanny ability to get under people's skin so effortlessly. He never fancied himself an asshole but accepted the fact that most people considered him a smug son-of-a-bitch. It was the reason he became a lawyer. For Wesley, getting what he wanted was always his goal and the price was never too high. At this point in his life it was too late to change now. He'd always been taught that only the strong, with a hint of conniving, survive. So, when J.J. took his position at the firm and the partners were coveting him as their golden boy, Wesley decided he needed some insurance for the future.

After spending time at his home and watching his relationship with Desiree, it was too easy to tempt him. Wes hired an escort service to lure J.J. but with such a delicate situation he needed the best. The woman who ran the operation would surely know how to seduce discreetly. No matter which way things turned out he'd always have ammunition to use against J.J.; lunch with an escort, dinner with an escort, sex with and escort. It was too good to be true. Surely the partners and his wife would frown on such scandalous behavior.

As Wes turned corner after corner he imagined how much he'd bask in the glorious moment that was sure to come. He just needed the right moment to use it. Although it was quite brisk out, Wesley rolled down his window and let the breeze chill his face. Today was a good day. He confirmed what he already knew; Lady K. was a true pit bull in a skirt.

∞ ∞ ∞

I spent the afternoon with James. It was a nice and pleasant date. He called early that morning to ask me to take a walk with him. I agreed. The leisurely stroll felt like our first date. We talked about nothing and it was the most fascinating conversation we'd had in months. I asked how his parents were doing and how work was going. He asked me how it felt to be a semi-bachelorette again and although we laughed that one off it had a serious tone to it. He held my hand and told me he loved me and that I was still the only woman he could ever love. The phone rang repeatedly with a number. He would look at it, then silence it until I finally asked, "Are you gonna answer? Someone really wants to get a hold of you." Moments later the phone rang again. "You'd better see what's on fire J.J." He pulled out his phone and took a few steps away from me.

"Are you home?"

"No. What's up?"

"Oh...I really need to talk to you . When are you gonna be there?"

"Not sure," he said trying to lower the volume.

"Ok...well...call me when you get there. We need to talk," the female voice on the other end of the line insisted. He ended the call and looked over at me.

"Everything ok?" I asked in a soft voice.

"Yeah," he answered nonchalantly.

∞ ∞ ∞

James walked into The Winery Restaurant and looked around. He approached the hostess and asked, "Do you have a reservation for James Taylor?"

"Let me see," the young brunette said scrolling the reservation book with her index finger. "Yes, I do. Party of two?"

"Sure," James said looking around.

"Right this way. Your party is already seated." James followed the young woman to a small room in the back of the restaurant. "Here you are. Tony will be right with you."

"Thank you," James replied before taking a seat on the opposite side of the table.

"I've taken the liberty of ordering our favorite," Lady K said as she poured a glass for James. "You remember, don't you James, Fetzer Gewurztraminer," she reminded him as she finished pouring.

"Yes. I do," James said seriously. "What is this all about? What was so important that you needed to meet me?"

Lady K. was poised and patient. She was clothed in an all black wrap around dress that plunged at the neckline ever so slightly and purple heels that matched her accessories to a tee. She crossed her legs and cleared her throat before she spoke, "I'm here on business and business only," she started. "I don't usually do this. To be honest, I don't usually care. However, you are a special case. So listen very closely to what I'm about to tell you, your career depends on it."

"Did you bring me here to blackmail me?" James asked through clinched teeth.

"No you idiot. But for a lawyer, you are shockingly naive," she noted. "I brought you here to tell you that you and I were no accident. A man named Wesley, who works at your firm, has got it out for you and he hired me to make sure that happened."

"What do you mean 'hired you'? And how do you know Wesley?"

"Like I said, listen. I was paid to seduce you. And I'm going to be paid to make sure everyone knows it. Your colleague has his eye on you and your position and he wants it bad," she said uncrossing her legs as she took a sip of wine. "Now, let me be clear. The only reason I am here, the only reason I am telling you any of this is because I've worked with a lot of scumbags in my day but Wesley....he is a different kind of scumbag. There is something more sinister to him than meets the eye. Plus I don't take kindly to sophomoric games when it comes to me and my business."

"I'm listening," James said.

"I don't give a care about your pretty boy perfect world. But what I do care about is sticking it to this S.O.B. who thinks he has any power over me and mine. He's so smart he's stupid! Kinda like you." She took another sip from the glass.

"What's your plan and what is it that you

want from me?" James asked curiously.

"He owes me another $20K when he is ready to embarrass you and its due 24-hours prior to his big reveal. So....I'm going to give you a discount because half the fun in this will be strictly for my amusement. $5K from you and I will deny it all and I will do to him what he is trying to do to you."

"$5,000 and that's it. No additional requests. You will disappear."

"Yes," Lady K smiled. "And just to show you that I'm such a good sport, I will defer payment until after the big show."

James sat back in his chair and studied the vixen in black for a moment. "You've got a deal," he said reluctantly.

"Good. Now it's impolite to let a girl drink alone. Pick up that glass and toast. *To us and the big reveal!*"

12
FRANKLY

My stomach was in knots while I drove up the side street toward Ray's house. I wasn't sure why my nerves were doing such a job on me. For the past two weeks we spoke on the phone daily. Our conversations were like that of familiar friends as well as star crossed lovers. I felt like I was getting to really know him for the first time and I liked the person being presented before me. Oddly enough we seemed to be in tune with each other and that was refreshing. I'd already promised myself that there would be no sex of any kind when I agreed to this visit. Not to mention politely informing him of the same. He assured me that sex was the furthest thing from his mind. Although I must admit I was slightly anxious about the fact that we hadn't talked about all of the serious things that needed to be said. Things like the baby, Tina, my marriage, and James.

When I arrived at Ray's house, I pulled into the driveway and like déjà vu he opened the front door and stepped onto the porch. He greeted me with a warm hug then kissed me on the cheek as he welcomed me inside. I walked into Ray's living room and noticed a new painting placed on the wall. I immediately gasped when I noticed the canvass image of myself from the night of the gala. There I was in all my white and red glory bigger than life over the mantel.

"Where did you get this? How?" I asked both confused and impressed.

"I told you, you were a work of art," he said with a smile.

My eyes were wide when I turned and looked at him in disbelief. I wasn't sure whether to be flattered or concerned. I mean the painting was quite elegant and made me admire myself like an art gallery exhibit. It was stunning but on the other hand, why would he take a snap shot of me and have it made to match the art in his home. That reeks of obsession, but like I said I was impressed, flattered, and disturbed all at that same time. I was a work of art! His adoration was beyond my comprehension. I knew he had feelings for me even if he did hide them under lock and key and kept them close to his chest. I turned and looked back at the image on the wall and nodded.

"Come here. Please, sit down," he asked overly confident.

"Sure," I said slowly, still pondering his motives behind the image on the wall. *Had Ray become a serial killer and forgot to tell me?* I thought to myself as I took my seat next to him, never taking my eyes off of it.

"Does it bother you?"

"I'm not sure. I'm trying to decide," I said slightly turning my head in his direction but keeping my eyes on myself.

"The photographer of the evening showed me some pictures and I just thought this really captured the essence of you. I call it, *Desiree's Delight*."

"*Desiree's Delight*, huh?" I smiled at the sentiment.

"Yes. From your smile I assume you now approve."

"Approved, Mr. Humphrey," I said finally looking into his eyes. "Thank you for such adoration." He took my hand in his and kissed it.

"Only one woman has ever stolen my heart and for that reason alone she deserves such a grand gesture," he said sincerely.

"I don't know what to say....Thank you."

"Now that that's out of way, how have you been?"

"I'm doing well," I answered quickly.

"You said that entirely too fast," he chuckled. "Was that the truth or a little nervousness speaking?"

"Both."

"I see. I told you on the phone that I just wanted to talk to you face to face. Nothing to be nervous about. I almost feel bad that you can't be comfortable around me anymore," he said repositioning himself to face the mantel. Ray took a deep breath and leaned back against the red mesh S-curved sofa complete with two silk pillows. I placed my hand on his thigh in an attempt to reassure him that whatever he needed to say was okay. He placed his hand over mine and swallowed hard."I have something to say and I need you to hear me out. Do you think you can do that?"

"Yes. Of course I can. We've been through a

lot already. What else can there be?" I asked with uncertainty.

"At some point you became my everything," he began then stopped. "I know there is a lot we need to discuss and a lot of things that have gone unsaid. I want to be one hundred percent honest with you Desi." He looked at me in a failed attempt to hold back the tears welling up in his eyes. "I miss you. The second you walked through that door I felt whole again. I'm tired of playing games. I miss you, love you. I want to know what are you gonna do? No games."

"Ray," I began before he stopped me.

"We had some moments Desiree Elizabeth, here me out, please. I thought you were supposed to have my baby. What happened?"

I took a deep breath and whispered, "You didn't want it."

"You didn't give me a chance to react...to fix it. I'm sorry for the way I reacted. Of course I wanted my child. How could you even think I didn't?"

"I lost it," I said feeling cornered.

"I hate that this went this way...that this happened to us...to you." He paused before continuing. "Can I ask what caused the miscarriage?" he asked without shifting his eyes from mine.

My face burned with remorse. My mind went back to the day I laid on the floor and bled. I couldn't answer....I couldn't tell him.

"You don't have to talk about it right now," Ray assured me.

"You didn't want it," were the only words that would escape my lips. "You didn't want it," I repeated.

"No matter what, you were always gonna go back to your husband. You even called me his name. How could I compete with that?"

No response was needed, so I said nothing.

"Fine. Don't respond." Ray's defenses were going back up. "Next time you see me..."

"Next time I see you what Ray?" I snapped back.

"Wait. Stop. That's not what I mean. This is hard enough for me to be this vulnerable in front of you...just bare with me," he said in a desperate attempt to return the conversation to its original purpose.

"I have a question." I said matter-of-factly. "Why were you sleeping with my best friend?"

"Tina? I wasn't sleeping with Tina. Where did you come up with that? Is that what she told you?" Ray asked stunned.

"Stop lying Ray! I saw you with her and your special 'friend'." I said using air quotes.

"Don't believe everything you see."

"Are you kidding me!" I said defensively.

"No. I'm not. I never slept with that girl!" Ray yelled. "What kind of man do you think I am?"

"Obviously I don't think very highly of you right now."

"So why are you here? Why did you come?"

"Because we needed to get some things out in the open. And I needed to look you in the eyes and find out why you hurt me like you did. And why you are trying so hard to come back into my life. *That's* why I'm here."

Ray stood up and went over to the window before responding. His emotions were up and down. He was happy I was sitting in front of him but pissed at my accusations. "Listen to me very carefully, Desiree, I *never* had sex with Tina. *Never.* No offense but that's one trifling woman," he stressed.

"I saw you Ray. C'mon you can do better than that," I said standing. "If you can't be honest with me then there is no reason for me to even be here."

Ray knew he would have to tell me the whole story sooner or later if he ever wanted that stain removed from my mind. "Ok, I'll tell you what happened but I need you to keep an open mind about all of this. Okay?"

I swallowed hard and took my seat moreover I prepared myself to listen to what was sure to be the tale to end all tales. Ray began to tell his side of the story.

13
YOU, ME & SHE

Tina steadied herself on Ray's massive bed. This was the night she'd been waiting on; she finally would get the chance to experience Ray's allegedly massive penis for the first time. Girl X had done the impossible! When they pulled up to the address on the GPS Tina was nervous. She wasn't sure what to expect from this rendezvous, she hadn't done this since college. Girl X assured her that she wouldn't be disappointed because the sex partner they were going to meet was very skilled and well endowed. With a quick kiss on the cheek Girl X rang the doorbell. To Tina's surprise Ray was the man that opened the door. Her excitement was barely contained.

"Well *hello* Tanya," Ray said taken aback at Girl X and her guest. He didn't usually call Girl X by her birth name but decided that formalities were in order until he could fully assess the situation.

"Hi there!" Tanya said stepping into the house; Tina followed. "This is my friend Tina. Tina this is my friend Ray."

"Yes, I know, we've met," Tina said looking into Ray's eyes.

"Yeah," was the only word Ray could utter. The look of confusion swept across his face as he looked over at Tanya.

"How do you two know each other?" Tanya questioned.

"She's a friend of a friend," Ray responded looking back at Tina.

"That I am," Tina said with a smirk.

"Oh...well...if this is going to be a problem just let me know," Girl X explained.

"Oh no. No problem at all," Tina said, feeling the moisture gather in her sweet spot.

"Uh...I'm not so sure," Ray objected.

"Wait...how exactly do you know each other again?" Tanya asked suspiciously.

"My best friend, Desiree, knows him *very* well," Tina said turning to look at Tanya.

"Oh," Girl X said watching the reactions on her playmates faces.

"I hate to disappoint you, I really do but I think I'm going to sit this one out."

"Why? Desiree and I have no secrets," Tina smiled like a cat with a canary in its mouth. "Unless...the two of you have something going on."

"I'm just not comfortable with this," Ray said to Tanya.

"Well if that's how you feel then you don't have to participate...but...would you mind being our muse? We came all the way over here," Tanya said pouting as she rubbed Rays arm.

"You are a real piece of work," he glanced at Tina.

"Isn't she!" Tina responded.

Ray took a moment to consider the request and agreed. "Alright. Just your muse. Nothing more."

"Great!" Girl X kissed Ray on his lips. "And it's ok if you change your mind," she took Tina by the hand and moved around Ray. Tina's eyes were fixed on him and her expression read trouble.

The immaculately polished spiral dark hardwood floors and white walls that led to the landing at the top of the stairs and right into Ray's bedroom flowed like an intoxicating trance. The ample anticipation of what was awaiting anyone who crossed that threshold was filled with so much pornographic promise that you could cum from just the walk alone. Ray stood at the bottom of the stairs and listened as the two seductive divas giggled their way into his bedroom. He could hear the sound of heels being tossed to the floor and the shower running. The feeling in the pit of his stomach began to churn as he tried to figure a way out of this mess. Ray in no way wanted or even desired Tina. Nor did he ever want Desiree to find out that Tina was ever at his place to do what she came to do. He quickly tossed around a few scenarios where this would end well for him but nothing good came to mind. Ray waited a little bit longer before heading up the stairs. He reluctantly followed the pair upstairs into his bedroom.

When he reached the door to his bedroom, he looked at the clothing strewn about the floor leading to bathroom. The door was open and he could see the ladies moving about as if the other was a decadent treat, waiting to be had. As he passed by the dresser he picked up a remote control and pressed the red power button. The sleek floating dark wooden shelves on the wall held a speaker on each. The red light blinked on each, one at a time and music began to flow through the room at a low volume. Next he clicked a switch on the wall near the bathroom door once, and then twice, the lights on the modern ceiling fan came up dramatically slow until the light was even across the room.

Tina entered the steamy shower hand-in-hand with Girl X. They began to French kiss under the water as Tina's hands began to explore Girl X's body. Tina started at her shoulder where she gently massaged them then traced her silhouette stopping at Girl X's hips. Tina took a handful of her butt and squeezed as Girl X pressed her tongue deeper into Tina's mouth. The wave of excitement and anticipation of what was to follow made both women moan. Girl X gripped the back of Tina's neck and Tina moved her hands slowly around her thighs and paused. Sliding her hands upward, Tina used her two thumbs to rest in the fold of Girl X's hips before using her right thumb to enter the split between Girl X's legs. Tina stroked her clit back and forth with medium force then pressed until she felt the response that she was aiming for; Girl X's clit pressed back. Tina began to rub the responsive pearl between her thumb and index finger as Girl X's body arched backwards. The pair stopped long enough to look at each other when they noticed Ray standing at the door of the bathroom watching. He crossed his arms and legs and leaned against the door.

For Girl X, her focus was Tina. For Tina, her focus was Ray. For Ray, his focus was on how to enjoy the night without actually having sex with either of the wet vixens in front of him. Tina returned her attention to Girl X and licked her earlobe while squeezing and pulling her clit. She could see Ray's member growing with interest even if his mouth was reluctant. Who can't resist two fine freaks in a shower? Girl X's moans broke Tina's thought and she slid two fingers inside Girl X and wiggled them. To Tina's delight, Girl X began to squeeze her own breasts as she closed her eyes. Tina dropped to her knees and shoved her rather long tongue into Girl X's crease, squeezing her thighs with her thumbs. "Oh yes." Girl X finally spoke as she reached for the towel rack inside the shower. Tina raised her leg and rested it on her shoulder to allow access to the moist opening of Girl X's center. Tina closed her eyes and imaged Ray tasting her the same way. She moaned through the licks and flicks and buried her face deeper into Girl X's thighs. Girl X mocked Tina's motion and Ray began to tug at his hardening package.

"You like riding her face?" He finally spoke.

"Yeeessss!" Girl X let out with a pant.

"I think you'd get a better feel for it if you give Tina a taste of what you can do." Ray said walking out of the bathroom into his bedroom. Tina took the hint and abruptly stopped. She looked up at Girl X and smiled, "After you." She said then licked her lips.

"I'm going to devour you," Girl X said helping Tina up.

"Like I said, after you."

Tina's honey pot throbbed with an immense pulse as she followed Girl X to Ray's bed. The massive black wooden king sized bed was draped in silver and black bedding while the large, firm pillows were covered in black cotton sleeves. She hoisted herself on one side and laid on her back. Girl X pushed her knees aside and dove in without hesitation. Tina was caught off guard by the biting sensation that radiated through her body but as she tilted her head to allow the sound of pained pleasure to escape, Ray placed a blind fold over her eyes. She smiled at his touch instead.

"Wait," He said "I almost forgot something."

"Awww Ray, I'm ready to play," Girl X said in a baby voice.

"Come with me," he said to Girl X.

"We'll be right back Tina," Girl X said moving away from the bed. Her bare breasts bounced along as she and Ray disappeared from the room. Tina sat up on her elbows and lifted the blindfold from her eyes. She looked around the room and tried to figure out where Ray would keep his condoms. She noticed the night stand and scouted to the side of the bed. She opened the drawer and there was a sleeve of six Magnum XL gold wrapped condoms. She took a bobby pin from her hair and pressed the pointed end into each of the six prophylactics. Ray pressed his hand against Girl X's naked abdomen to stop her from entering the room. He silently motioned for her to look at Tina, who was poking at the last two condoms on the row. He then pushed her back into the hallway and motioned for her to go back down stairs. A naked Girl X entered the kitchen first as Ray followed still wearing his tank top and maroon silk pajama bottoms.

"See!" I told you I didn't feel comfortable with this!" he whispered.

"Oh my god. I never would have thought she was *that* girl." Girl X whispered back covering her mouth.

"*That* girl is my girl's best friend!" Ray admitted.

"The girl that wanted the experiment?" Girl X questioned.

"*Yes!*" Ray answered emphatically.

"Why didn't you say so!"

"*Shhhh!* Keep your voice down. I was trying to but you weren't listening. I had *no* intentions of sticking my dick in any orifice she has."

"So you were going to leave me hanging?"

"No. I was going to use this shit to fuck with her a little and make her think she got me," Ray said holding out the honey and dildo in his hands. "So now you know my plan and you see why!"

"Okay. Okay. So let's stick to it then. I'm going to get what I came for."

"You better be lucky I like you," Ray said following Girl X out of the kitchen and up the stairs again.

As the pair re-entered the bedroom, they noticed Tina had reassumed her original position they'd left her in; blind folded and laying on her back.

"We're *baaack,*" Girl X sang.

"Oh good, you had me worried for a minute," Tina said nervously.

"Ahhh no, we weren't letting you off that

easy," Ray said looking at the neatly shaved mound between Tina's legs. Although he had no intentions of penetrating that manhole it still made his lower region jump to attention. "We just had to go get some little additions to our show and I needed an extra arm," Ray said in an attempt to sway the subject.

"*Oh* sounds sexy," Tina purred.

"Always," Girl X said winking at Ray.

"Have you ever heard of a sweet dick?" Ray asked.

"No," Tina said.

"Well, you have now," Ray said, "I'm going to lather this fat dick with honey and you are going to suck it until I go limp."

"Hmmm," Tina moaned. "Bring it here."

Before Tina could utter another word Girl X bit down on the vaginal lips and placed a self shifting vibrating bullet in her opening. "No more talking," Girl X commanded. She commenced flickering Tina's clit with the point of her tongue as Tina squirmed with pleasure. The sensation was almost unbearable. The short bursts of buzzing from the device mixed with Girl X's tongue caused a climax then stop sensation that resonated throughout her body as Ray disrobed and looked on.

Just when Tina thought she was going to explode Girl X nodded at Ray in a spreadable kneeling position at the top of Tina's head and they simultaneously slipped two honey lubed silicon dildos in each of Tina's last two openings; one in her mouth and the other in her anus. Tina's gagged scream made her body tense but she released when

Ray said, "Suck this dick 'til its limp and you can have it any where you'd like." Tina's jaws began to ferociously pump away at the toy resting between her lips as Girl X pumped the other in and out in opposing succession of the automatic joy stick being held in place by the walls of her vagina. Ray held the piece in place on an angle and pinched at one of Tina's nipples. He squeezed and slapped at them and made minimal noise to show he was fully engaged. He quickly withdrew the silicon dick and hit it on Tina's face and forehead before it dried out and placed it underneath the pillow and stated, "I'm bored with this."

"Me too," said Girl X as she pulled the dildo from Tina's anus.

"Huh? No. Why? I'm having so much fun," Tina said.

"Ray, what do you think?" Girl X asked.

"I don't know why you brought me this boring piece of ass."

"I'm not even hard anymore," Ray confessed.

Tina pulled the blindfold from over her eyes and turned to look at the limp meat resting between Ray's thighs and the automatic piece continued its mission. She seemed genuinely shocked that his erection was no longer.

"I know what I came for and I'm going to get it," Girl X said breaking the silence.

A confused Tina turned to look at her and then back at Ray. Ray slid the automatic piece from between Tina's thighs and instructed Girl X to lie on the bed while he removed his clothes. Once Girl X was on her back, Ray spread her legs slowly and rubbed the inside of her thighs while Tina looked on. He was almost at the insertion point when Girl X said, "Wait, shouldn't you put a condom on that thing?"

"Oh, I'm sorry," Ray said. "Tina, can you look in that top drawer and hand me those condoms."

Tina's eyes grew wide as she reluctantly opened the drawer and handed the string of condoms to Ray. *I can't believe this bitch would still hand me a rubber she poked a hole in to fuck another female with*, Ray thought.

This bitch is something else! Girl X thought, although slightly turned on at Tina's ruthlessness. Ray opened the golden wrapped condom and placed it over his wood. Then, to Tina's surprise, opened another and placed it over the automatic vibrator and swiftly inserted it into Girl X's opening and released it. He sat and watched it for a moment or two then instructed Tina to kiss and suck Girl X's nipples. Feeling like she was back in the game, Tina obliged. Ray rubbed Girl X's pearl with a pressured thumb until she came and he left the room. Tina's night was officially over.

14
FAVORS

"It's good to know people. It's even better to be respected by those people, because when you need a favor, they don't really ask too many questions or even flinch at whatever it is you're asking for," James thought to himself while sitting at lunch with Javán listening while he talked to Judge Gist. She was known for being a stern and powerful judge. Judge Gist rarely did favors for anyone but she'd always held a special place in her heart for Javán. I think it's because he used to date her daughter until she passed away from cervical cancer two years ago. He'd always planned to marry her but they never made it to the altar.

"Yes. Thank you. I completely understand," Javán responded effortlessly to the voice on the other end of the cell phone. James continued to sip the lemon water in front of him as he anxiously but patiently awaited the end of the call.

"Alright. I will send someone over today," Javán said giving J.J. the thumbs up. "I'll talk to you soon. Okay. Bye." Javán ended the call and sat back in his seat more satisfied than J.J.

"Well? What did she say?"

"She said you will have your warrant by this afternoon. She also said she is looking forward to dinner with us and your wife soon." He paused. "And she said she doesn't typically do these kinds of favors but because she knows us and trusts our judgment she will oblige this request *one* time and *one* time only."

"Great! Thanks man," James said sincerely.

"No problem. What are friends for?"

James felt good knowing what he was about to embark on came with such support, even if the supporters were blind participants. Nothing about this was right...except for the fact that this douche bag thought he could fuck with him and his wife and think James Jones Taylor was going to do nothing about it. J.J. was determined to restore order in this situation.

∞ ∞ ∞

I was laying flat on my stomach with my eyes closed. I didn't remember going to sleep. My hands touched something that my fingers wiggled around an object that felt sort of soft and squishy yet firm; like an earlobe. Without thinking, I instinctively spread my legs and pulled it toward my center. I started to rub the top of the thing; I felt it harden. Part of it pulled away from me but I pulled it back and let it go. My eyes remained closed. I adjusted myself, both legs spread; one leg bent while the other relaxed lazily in the long position. The movement in was swift in space. My hesitant participant changed his mind and went for it. I let out an *'ahhh'* only to be gagged by a penis that entered my mouth. My first instinct was to allow my tongue to work around the intrusion.

With my eyes wide shut and in what felt like

a drug induced haze, I realized I couldn't have one penis in my mouth and the other entering me below – that couldn't be the same penis, I mean person. I opened my eyes and tried to say *No. Stop. Wait.* Nothing came out however both pieces of man meat continued to penetrate me. I couldn't help but notice that the one in my mouth was fat. My eyes were blurry but I could make out three girls and a fully clothed man. They weren't watching what was happening to me. I was afraid to look around. The man behind me asked if I did this all the time to get ahead. I said, "No." That's when the voice coming from the man behind me suddenly sounded so familiar – the man behind me was my husband! James was allowing me to be violated while he participated. Not in my wildest dreams did I ever think…. "You're okay with this?" I said spitting out the all of a sudden vile penis in my mouth. He asked if this was what I wanted.

I choked and my heart raced as my body propelled itself forward from my sleeping position. I was drenched with sweat. I wiped my brows with both hands and wiped my neck from side to side. I was relieved to know it wasn't real; that I was dreaming. This wasn't the first or the last time that I'd have dreams like this.

∞ ∞ ∞

I situated myself on the chase lounge so that the pounding behind my right temple would fall to the back of my head. It didn't help much but any relief was better than none. My day had been awful and my life as a whole wasn't much better. I clasped my fingers over my eyes and began to cry.

"I can see from your body language, you're having a rough time today," Dr. Anirbas said curiously.

"Rough isn't even the word," I murmured.

"But you still managed to keep your appointment. That's good," she added.

"Maybe it is. Maybe it isn't."

"Care to explain?"

"I'm not sure how much this is helping me. I feel like things are just getting worse. I mean damn! I can do bad all by myself! All these damned emotions and being honest in the moment," I said mockingly, "is fuckin' with my head. I don't know who I am any more. Only confusion. That's all I know is confusion."

"Why is that?"

"Don't start that shit! Stop it!" I snapped with my fingers still interlaced over my eyes.

"The only way you are going to accomplish any kind of breakthrough is if you are honestly recognizing why things are the way they are."
I inhaled deeply and expelled all of the air in my lungs before I spoke. "It's confusing because it is. Because I'm always second guessing myself and wondering if I made the right decisions. I don't have a crystal ball so how in the hell can a person know for sure," I said drifting. My mind wondered to an image of J.J. smiling at me. Silence fell on my lips and my tears spoke volumes. I didn't even try to gather myself. I just cried the ugliest cry. I didn't allow anything to stop that flow and neither did Dr.

Anirbas. It felt good – no, great to let it out this way. My damaged self was ready for repair but not before I made a few more mistakes.

15
HAND JOBS ARE HIGH SCHOOL

"So you're seeing a shrink."

"Yes. I am. You've driven me officially crazy."

"I drove you crazy?" he laughed. "The last time I checked you were already crazy."

"I'm a special kind of crazy."

"You got that right!" he said walking into the closet. "So what do you do in there? Just walk in and lie on the couch and spill your guts?" he asked while removing his shirt.

"Come here and I will show you," I said taking his hand. "You will be my patient and I will be your therapist," I walked him over to the bed and sat him down. "Lay back and put your feet up."This will be sex therapy."

"Oh!" he said with an eyebrow raise.

"Yes. Now do as I ask. I'm the doctor remember."

"Whatever you say doc," He said as he placed his manicured feet on the bed. His bare chest toward the ceiling and his back against the white and red sheets made for a nice canvass. His white linen pants were unbuckled and slightly unzipped. I studied him for awhile in silence.

"*Sooo* what's next doc?"

"*Shhh.* Just relax your mind. Listen to the quiet," as I spoke he smiled and closed his eyes. "Take both hands and unzip your pants," I said softly.

"Ok."

"*Shhhh,*" I reminded him. "Now place one hand one your dick and pleasure yourself."

He opened one eye and peeked at me.

"Trust me. Pretend I'm not here. Listen to the quiet."

He did as I'd requested. Without moving his pants down any further he reached in his pants and pulled out the mass that was his manhood. His body was lighter than I remembered but his package was darker than I remembered too. It wasn't fully erect but it had the potential to blossom. He began to knead the head with his thumb while holding the shaft. I stood and watched intently for a few moments before I pulled the cushioned chair from the space next to the dresser. He began to enjoy his touch and started to move his hand up and down to a rhythm in his mind. I slowly stepped back until the back of my legs hit the chair that was now adjacent to the bed, where I sat down.

I stripped him naked as he lay on the bed and I spread his legs wide enough for his ball sack to drop. I noticed he'd tried to peek through closed lids, "Close your eyes," I requested. He obliged. I ran into the bathroom and retrieved the baby oil from the cabinet and assumed a kneeled position on the chair resting to the side of him. With his eyes sealed shut I rubbed my hands together to warm them, placed a dime sized amount of baby oil in the palm of my hand and rubbed them together again. I allowed my index finger to trace the center of his ball sack to the crack of his butt. His legs trembled slightly. I placed the palm of my hand around the shaft of his penis and gently squeezed. The tips of my fingers on my opposite hand found the warmest place between his thighs. I swiped the area gently a few times before I cupped the pair of oversized sacks awaiting their turn.

He moaned in a low sexy voice. I added a quarter sized amount of baby oil to my palm and rubbed them together again. I placed both hands on his shaft; one on top and the other at the base and began a virtual vaginal simulation complete with squishing sounds from the liquid. Up and down with a twist. All the way up to the head and blew. I could tell he was enjoying it by the way his body jerked uncontrollably and his squirms were attached to moans, but he never opened his eyes. I didn't need a special gel or massage oil to bring him to orgasm, just pure skill and the desire to get him to explore or revisit an old practice. Before I knew it he'd exploded in the air and it landed on my face, his chest, stomach, and my hands.

Without opening his eyes, he said, "A hand job huh?"

"I did it right. Who says hand jobs are just for high school," I simply replied with a big smile and semen resting on my face and hands. I rose and went to turn on the shower. I undressed quickly, hoping to remove any evidence of this experiment. *In and out. I will be done before he gets any ideas.*

At least that's the lie I told myself. As I stepped into the warm water Ray walked in; naked and sticky, he joined me.

I've heard a million times before how great sex can keep a bad relationship going for a long time. I used to think that was total BS…until now. What can I say, the body wants what it wants and my body wanted Ray. I can't ever tell if it's the sex or the anticipation that makes it so hot?! I refused to turn to look at him as the shower ran over my face. Then I heard him speak and I touched myself.

"Who am I?" Raymond asked in the sultriest deep voice.

"You are Raymond Humphrey. Anymore questions?" I replied sassily. He turned me around and asked again. This time my eyes couldn't hide from his. I couldn't joke my way out of answering his question.

"Who am I?"

"You are the man who divided my heart and ripped it out," I said honestly.

"I'm sorry for that," he said sincerely,

"Be sorry for nothing," I said with a sigh. My eyes redirected their focus to Ray's chest and all I could think was how much I just wanted him to hold me. How I just wanted to lie on his chest and feel safe again. "Do you love me?" I whispered before looking up at him again.

"I would be a fool not to love you," he said taking my face into his hands before giving me the softest most sincere kiss I'd had in a long time. No tongue. No lust. Just lips and love.

"This is crazy! I'm crazy!" I pulled away

from him. Once I did, I suddenly felt naked. I mean bare butt ass naked. Like my soul was standing between us and he could see everything. I planted my hand over the scars on my lower belly and tried to hide. He pushed them away and placed the palm of his hand over them. I looked down at his hand and a tear escaped from my eyes. I was happy the water from the shower spout was firm enough to cover up my accidental remorse.

"If I needed a doctor, you could be it," he rubbed his thumb over my blemish.

"Yes, I guess I could be her," I placed my hand over his and looked into his eyes. He backed me up into the corner of the shower and cupped my breast with both hands as he lowered himself. Ray rubbed my breasts as he pointed his tongue and slowly traced the outline of my orchid, taking special care to double lick the clit every time he landed there. I slid to the floor and completely gave in. He held my legs in the air like they were hooked to a levy.

"What's my name?!" he said slamming his massive organ into my tunnel. "Get it right this time," he continued holding my legs in the air. I screamed in delight but did not reply. There's something about the sound of skin slapping together that turns me on! Just the thought of a ball sack smacking against my special place sends me into a frenzy! He gyrated his hips in a counter clockwise motion. After each pound he gave me just enough time to respond. To his frustration I refused to cooperate.

16
NOTHING MATTERS

I hopped out of bed and made my way into the adjacent bathroom. I turned on the hot water and pulled the shower knob to allow the water to spring out. As the water began to warm the steam began to rise, I pranced my way into the living room. I flipped on the CD player and the soulful sound of Anthony Hamilton boomed throughout my place. I pulled the navy blue lace night slip over my head to reveal my nude body as I re-entered the bathroom and stepped in the shower. The combination of steam, suds and sounds made my feel good, alive and very sexy.

I sang along with the melody as I gently rinsed my body and turned off the water and stepped out. As I reached for the oversized soft cotton towel to dry myself I glanced at my own reflection in the frosty mirror. My skin was glowing. The dark contrasts of my areolas made me admire the size of my breast, but wish my lower midsection was tighter. With a mental note to work on my body, I sauntered back into the bedroom belting out the next track. I stopped in front of the dresser drawer to pick out a bra and panty combo that fit my mood. The coral and off white lace bra with coral and lace boy short panties seemed to make the right statement. I put them on in the full length mirror on the wall and began to sway my hips to the tune. I crossed one leg in front of the other, placed one hand on my hip, leaned forward and blew a kiss to myself. *"Damn I feel good!"* I said to no one. As I repositioned myself I walked backwards a few steps never taking my eyes off of my reflection. I stopped and whipped my arms across my body. With my knees bent I started to swirl my body toward the floor. As my body rested in a closed leg squat, I forced my knees open with my hands and posed for the pretend camera in front of me. I lifted my arms to the ceiling and one hand traced the other as I rolled my body up into a standing position. As the song neared its frenzied end I gave a bow to myself and strutted into the closet. The inside of my thighs ached with each flex. I hadn't realized how hard I'd been worked over until I attempted to cross my legs. Show over. Time to get ready for the day.

∞ ∞ ∞

Has your soul ever leapt out of your body after sitting on the edge of confusion for so long? Mine has! That's what it's doing right now. As soon as I walked into my therapist's office my blissful mood changed drastically. When I left my house this morning I really thought I'd finally figured it out, then bam! I was slapped in the face with the reality that I still hadn't been completely honest with Ray and I was certain he still wasn't being one hundred percent honest with me as the good doctor pointed out.

I explained my last few encounters with Ray, my shower this morning, the music, the dancing, and how all of those things were great feelings. She looked at me and handed me a piece of paper and pen and told me to write a letter to my other self, like something I would tell a friend or another young lady going through something. The album in my head was on rotation and I began to write;

DESIRE vs. DESIREE
Letter to my ladies:
Ever wonder why music is so powerful especially when you are in a relationship that is facing problems? It's because songs speak to your situation. Yep! They actually help you make decisions about your life! Life and death decisions! Take a minute and think about it. It you're in a relationship that's not going great...let's say he cheats on you (yeah like my situation) and you've been in each other's life since before you can remember, you'll listen to songs about cheating and forgiveness because you've been in a relationship with that person for forever and they made one mistake. A mistake that hurt like hell but a mistake no less. So you get angry, cry, swear you're through and then go back when he says, "Babe babe please. I'm sorry."

Then you have those relationships where someone disrespects you, cheats repeatedly, hits you, steals from you, calls you names and other unspeakable wrongs so you listen to songs about being strong, leaving, emotional and even the ones

*that claim that's how life goes. Then you listen to
the take them back that's how life goes songs until
they say, "babe babe please." Not even an apology
to you but because of your history you go back and
it starts all over again and again and again and you
call it love.*

*I hate the cycle. I hate seeing my friends or
family go through that. What's more, I hate it when
I go through it but I'm too blind or stupid to know
that's what's happening. Well, I finally learned my
lesson and it's time to spread the good news;
Ladies, just because a man desires you doesn't
mean he values you. When this valuable realization
finally hit me I cried. I cried for myself and every
young lady and woman out there that doesn't know
the difference. I also cried when I realized my name
was right smack in the middle of this foolishness.
Right there! Take a look! Ladies, just because a
man DESIRES you doesn't mean he values you. See
that? The base of my name DESIRE.*

On the last stroke of my pen, I cried even
harder. Dr. Anirbas handed me tissues and rubbed
my back. Have you ever wondered what the
soundtrack to your life would be? Have you ever
given it any thought? Would it be filled with drama,
action, rock, jazz, or love ballads? I think mine
would be filled with a lot of *'dun dun dun'*!
However what I'd like is a lot more orchestra...more
symphony but I don't seem to get it. I've never been
a bad friend or lover or even a bad person. I think
I'm just misunderstood.

I blame a lot of it on my mother. She was
always in competition with me. So that's what I

always thought, women are always in competition. I don't like losing but for that matter who does. Okay maybe I really can't blame my mom but isn't that what people do in therapy? Isn't that usually the answer? I'd had enough of this session. My bed was calling me.

17
DIRT FREE

I was lying in bed staring at the ceiling trying to figure out life again. A lot has happened and things can't get any worse; at least in my opinion. You know that saying, *"eyes are the soul"*. It's true. Not everybody has the gift to look into someone's eyes and tell if they are real, genuine, or filled with the Holy Spirit or even worse, the devil-- not everyone. Even those with the gift can be fooled from time to time. I'd always considered myself one of those people but I was sure I'd been fooled this time. Every time I close my eyes I see his eyes just staring back at me. I can't read them. That means he's good at deception. I open my eyes and stare at the ceiling...that's deception.

I had to call Raymond. I needed to get this out once and for all. One thing was for sure and two was for certain; I don't know why it was so damned important for me to tell him because I'd already confessed to GOD but if I was going to restart my life over again and do it right, everything had to be out in the open. My phone rang and I answered abruptly.

"Hello."

"Hey girl! How you doing?" Tara asked ever so sweetly.

"I'm fine. How are you?"

"On cloud nine but that's a conversation for another day. What are you doing?"

"Lying down at the moment. Wait, cloud nine? Island man is still around?"

"Yeah," Tara said with a giggle. "Are you sure you're ok? I haven't heard from you."

"Yep. I'm good. By the way, thanks for the therapist suggestion. It's really been working out."

"You are like a sister to me. I've always got your back."

"Hey listen, I've got to go talk to Ray today and I think I might need your shoulder later. Are you busy?"

"If I was, I'm not now. Just call me."

"Thanks for being a great friend! I love you dearly!" I smiled.

"*Muah!* Good luck."

"I'm going to need it. The weird thing is, I shouldn't be this nervous but I am."

"You'll feel better after you get it off your chest."

"I'm sure you're right. Okay I gotta go."

"Bye," Tara sang.

"Bye," I sang back.

∞ ∞ ∞

Javán and James pulled into the precinct parking lot where detective Bryant Rowe was waiting for him. James handed him an envelope containing some paperwork. They chatted a bit about family, life, and the American dream before J.J. signaled Javán that it was time to leave.

"Thanks again for saving me the trip into the building," Javán said as he shook detective Rowe's hand. "Judge Gist asked me to deliver it personally on my way home."

"It's been a good day for me," James interjected. "I think I'll take the wife out for dinner tonight," Javán looked in J.J.'s direction.

"Alright fellas. Let me know when we are hitting the court again. I could use a quick win," Detective Rowe waved and laughed.

∞ ∞ ∞

"What happened to my baby?" Raymond asked firmly.

Shocked at the directness of his question and the tone of his voice, I turned my head cautiously in his direction.

"What took you so long to ask?" I said calmly.

"I was waiting for you to just tell me yourself but I see that's not going to happen," he said with conviction. "I'm tired of waiting for you to bring it up."

"Ray..." I responded with a look of desperation. "I really don't want to talk about this right now."

"You owe me an answer Desiree!"

"No, Ray, actually I don't," she said matter-of-fact.

"Yes you do!" The growl in his voice was quickly becoming fiery anger. "According to you that was my child. I have a right to know what happened to my child!"

"You mean the child that you said you didn't want. The same child that made you act like you didn't know my name. *That* child?!" My words were shots Ray hadn't been prepared to take.

"No matter what I said," Ray chose his words carefully, "I still have a right to know what ultimately happened."

"I lost it," I said flatly and coldly.

"When? How?" He said sitting down. "I'm so sorry I made you go through that alone."

"Not too long after our fight. After you said you didn't want it," I started to explain with tears in my eyes. "It doesn't matter how. Just know I'm not a mother. The whole entire situation was screwed up."

Raymond sat in silence although he wanted to ask more questions. Waiting and wanting me to give him more detail. He watched as a few large tears dropped from my eyes. *She looks so tormented. I didn't know whether to wipe her tears, hug her or let her work through*, Ray thought as he watched. "I'm sorry," was all he could muster. "That must have been hard."

I nodded a slow yes and he wiped my eyes with the palm of his hand. "You have no idea."

"If it helps, I want you to know that I would do it differently if I had the chance....if I could turn back time." He looked down, clasped his hands together and rested his forearms on his knees.

"It doesn't."

A tear dropped from his eyes and landed on the white carpet. I hadn't realized I was getting so emotional until then. "How are you coping with the miscarriage?"

"Who says I am? And who says it was a miscarriage?" I hollered.

"I wanted to be there for you. I honestly did. Is there anything I can do now?"

"Too little, too late," I said staring through him. A chill went through Ray's body when our eyes connected. His anger had calmed and mine became almost deadly. I was getting that annoying heat in my nose and face when you're about to cry. You know the one; the stinging in my eyes, the lump in my throat when I tried to swallow hard. My head told me to be strong but my heart was screaming to let it all out. I trembled because the internal struggle was too much for my physical body so it started to visibly shake. Anger and sadness collided.

"I'm sorry but what do you mean, who says it was a miscarriage? How else could you lose a baby?" Ray questioned as I grabbed my things and prepared to walk toward the door. He shot after me and begged me to stay and finish the conversation but I wasn't having it. This was not going the way I had planned.

"Those marks on my belly are because I made the decision to remove any part of you from me! Do you get it now?!"

"What?!"

"You heard me! I didn't lose your child Ray! I got rid of it for you!"

"Are you crazy?! How? You could have killed yourself!"

"That was the plan!" I shouted through a tsunami of tears.

Ray released me without another word. "Go," he said in disbelief. "You need some time...I need some time." There was nothing further that either of us could say that would change the situation anyway.

"You stripped me of my life, my space, my virtue, and I allowed it. I gave you permission when I believed you!" I slapped his face. "No more!"

18
EPIPHANY

Saturday morning came by so quickly. I awoke lying on the couch in my living room in my apartment. Thursday night's fight with Raymond had yielded three rounds of screaming and finger pointing and no resolutions. Once I'd left his place I found myself walking in a haze of confusion. The rest is literally a blur. I'm not even going to question how I ended up back here.

Once again, it was time to deal with me. To be honest, I was tired of me. I was tired of being weak. I was tired of being the girl with the problems. I sat there trying to figure out why I did this to myself. True it started with James Jones Taylor but it was ending with me. I thought I'd lost J.J. so I think I figured I'd try my luck with Raymond. But I hadn't lost J.J. at all; I'd lost myself. He made a mistake and I've been hanging it over his head for too long. The hurt came and set up shop like this temporary apartment and I never asked it to leave. I was holding on to it as my ultimate excuse to do whatever it was that I pleased.

Why should I go on punishing him? I didn't want to train another man at this stage in my life. Hell, I don't even know myself anymore. I've learned lessons the hard way before but this was extreme even for me! Was I a glutton for punishment? I guess two wrongs really don't make a right. There goes another damn cliché again. My silent reflections became verbal reminders of all the lessons I'd learned the first time around. I picked up the phone and dialed. It was time for damage control.

My voice was strong and weak. "Can you come?" I asked.

"Why?"

"Because."

"Why?"

"I need you....I need you to see me for who I am now, not who I used to be."

"Why?"

"Stop asking why and come."

"No."

"*No?*"

"No."

I didn't know how to respond, so I waited.

"*Hello?*"

"Yes."

"Anything else?"

"No."

"Do you understand?" he asked curiously.

"Understand what?"

"I already see you for *who* you are. I don't need to come to you for that reason."

"What are saying?"

"I'm saying, the reason why should be because you love me Desiree. Because you love *me* and you need *me* to know that you love *me*."

"If you would just come to me James, you

will get all of that."

"The better question is; do I want it?"

"What?" I asked shocked by such an assertion. "Stop it."

"Stop what? You aren't the only one that gets to ponder life and our relationship Desi."

"You are doing this to hurt me. That's not fair, seeing as you started this ball rolling in the first place," I said in a low growl as tears welled in the corner of my eyes.

"I may have started it but you kept running with it. I made one mistake a long time ago and you want to punish me for it for the rest of my life. I won't allow you to do that. You can make a mess of things for yourself, not for both of us," J.J. said with conviction.

"And now I'm ending it," I said defeated.

"Then...I will come."

"*Really?*" I asked with a sigh of relief.

"Really," he answered.

"Thank you."

"No, thank you." he said with a smile. "I love you."

"I love you too," I repeated. "Hang up and get here."

"Right now?" J.J. answered nervously. "I can't right now...um...I'm in the middle of something important. Not that anything is more important than you. I just can't right now."

"Oh, you're right. I have something I need to do anyway. I will see you tomorrow evening."

∞ ∞ ∞

"So tell me about your last dream," Dr. Anirbas started.

"My last dream...huh...." I drew my head back in the seat and thought. "It was one I'd like to forget. I woke up very angry."

"What happened that made you so angry? Can you describe it?" the doctor asked again.

"James had asked me to come over for a visit, I declined. I changed my mind and went anyway. When I got there, the door was unlocked but when I tried to open the door I couldn't because there was a chain connected on the other side. I heard J.J. say *'Who is it?'* from the other side and I announced myself. I could see through the opening that he was naked. He told me to hold on, and when he finally opens the door, he hurries me over to the couch in the living room. He's acting very suspicious and wants my eyes focused on him. Then I hear something in the bedroom, so I rush toward the door and bust it open. There was a woman wrapped in bed sheets standing there. I immediately go into animal psycho mode. James picks me up in one of those fisted bear hugs and that's when I remember; it's not her fault he's a lying, cheating, dick. It's his. So I start punching him all over his body. I was screaming for him to put me down and he eventually did. That's when I walked outside and set his car on fire."

"Interesting dream."

"Yeah. It's pretty obvious what that was all

about," I said sarcastically. "No need to psychoanalyze that one."

"You think so?"

"A blind man could see where that was going," I laughed.

"*Mmmhmm* just like the last one?" she asked curiously.

"Well...yes."

"We rely on dreams to keep us going and become sad when they tear us down," the doctor advised. "Do you think your dream represents the loss of your marriage? We haven't really talked about loss or grief at any length. Do you notice you usually change the subject?" Dr. Anirbas challenged.

"I don't fear life. I don't even fear death because I know it's inevitable," I paused. "I live life like it's a marathon and I need to score as many points as possible before I cross the finish line," I said turning my head to look in her direction. "Ya know it's funny....so many people around me mourn and I actually mourn for them. Not even for myself but for them. I worry about how they will handle whatever tragedy they are facing," I took a deep breath and thought about my brother, Derrick. "I cry real tears...sometimes I just weep at the possibility of it all. Love and loss, those are necessary thorns of life. Like Derrick...."

"Detaching from your feelings doesn't work; it only leads to a lonely existence."

"But it's worked for me for so long. I don't know any other way. Funny thing about life, we hate for wrong to be done to us but will still do it to someone else. I do know one thing, if this was just sex, it would be easy to walk away from all the madness. If I didn't have so much to lose it would be really easy. It would be so easy," I repeated absent mindedly. "But what I do know is that I can't stand myself for it. It's not fair and I don't know what to do."

"What's not fair?"

"That I don't know how to make him talk to me; to listen to what I *don't* know because I don't even know where to begin. All I know is this shit! I can't stop crying and it hurts like hell and I have to just get over it because that's what people do, right, they get over it."

19
WAGED WAR

Ray had a lot to think about after I dropped the bomb about what really happened to our love child. Ray didn't want a child, and yes he'd told me to get rid of it, but the thought of killing a child by my own hand did something to him. But how could Ray be mad? I think the thought that this strong woman was that emotionally unstable made him cringe. If I could harm myself and an unborn child that way what else was I capable of? Ray kept going back to the fact that he asked me to have an abortion. He rationalized that I'd just gone about it a different way. *Doesn't make sense does it.* It's the same thing, isn't it?

He hated to think that he caused me that much hurt that I'd do this! *Nah, that can't be my fault. She must've had a few screws loose already. Sad thing is; she is just my kind of crazy.* He contemplated as he drove along. Ray hopped in his car and took the long way to my place. The drive felt long and tedious. Ray seemed to pass every single family in the neighborhood laughing and smiling and enjoying each other. He wanted that and decided the he was finally willing to make it happen.

Ray pulled up to my building and parked his

car but didn't get out. He took a moment to really assess if he wanted to go through with this whole relationship. He must've sat there too long because an officer pulled up alongside him and asked what he was doing. "Waiting on my girlfriend," Ray said without hesitation. The officer nodded and advised him not to loiter, so Ray got out and went to the door and rang the buzzer marked *D. Taylor*.

"Who is it?"

"Ray."

"Ray who?"

"Ray, the man who is here to make things right."

"Ray? I don't know anyone by that name."

"Desiree stop playing. Come down here."

"No."

"*No?*"

"No. You come up."

"Then let me in."

Buzz

Ray entered the foyer of the building and was greeted by a large mosaic table which held the largest crystal vase of multicolored roses he'd ever seen. They were a nice accent and very calming. Ray looked around. "*I must admit my girl has great taste,*" he said aloud. Everything included white, yellows and splashes of red. Ray pressed the elevator button and when the doors opened, I stepped out. I greeted me with a kiss on the cheek and without saying a word I walked out the door he'd just walked in. It was his turn to follow behind me like a puppy with a scurried walk, trying to beat me to the car door. I made it there before Ray and politely waited for him to open the car door. Once inside Ray suggested that we just take a drive and talk. He pulled away from the curb and began what felt like a labored conversation.

"So...." Ray said with a deep breath, "how are you?"

"Fine. I'm doing just fine."

"Our last visit didn't end well."

"I know."

"So do you want to talk about it?"

"Do you?"

"Yes, I do," Ray replied quickly.

"Do you think this is necessary?"

"You don't think it is?"

"Well have at it then," I said a little too calmly for his taste.

"Woman you are a thorn in my side," Ray said glancing over at me. "I've been doing a lot of thinking and I think we owe each other an apology."

"*Pfft*." I scoffed, not really amused by his statement.

"We do. I've done some wrong and you've done some *crazy* wrong but somehow we seem to work."

"You think so."

"Yes, I do," Ray said ignoring my sarcasm and continued with his thought. "Would you leave him...for me...for good this time?" The question was slow and purposeful.

"I-I...." I took a deep breath remembering my conversation with J.J. mere hours before. "I don't want to hurt anybody but I'm hurting everybody," was my honest response.

"That doesn't answer the question."

"No it doesn't."

"I'm going to say it again."

"Please don't. You don't have to. I heard you."

"So answer the –"

"I love you –"

"Answer –"

"Let me finish Ray. I love you but I don't know if I can trust you. I love him and he is trying to work things out between us. I don't want to screw up two lives with uncertainty."

"You love me but you're not sure if *you* can trust *me?*" he repeated.

"Yes. I keep thinking of what might have been and what could be. With all that has happened between us you can't forget the fact that you slept with my best friend."

"That's all you got!"

"That's enough isn't it?"

"You're a married woman having an affair with *me* and *you're* mad that I slept with someone else. Man Desi, you've got nerve!"

"It wasn't just some other girl! She was my BEST FRIEND!"

"Some friend," he shook his head as he pulled over.

"This conversation is over Ray!"

"Oh no it isn't!" Ray said grabbing Desiree's wrist.

"I'm giving you three seconds to take your hands off of me," Desiree said in the calmest and collected voice she could muster. "That is the *second* time you've thought it was ever ok to grab me and if it ever crosses your mind again...consider yourself warned."

"Wait. I'm sorry. I don't know how else to get you to sit still and deal with what's in front of us. Please don't go," Ray said releasing my wrist. I rubbed the spot that he'd held. "I don't want to keep doing this. I want to show you something that will put this Tina business to rest. Then you can get back to all of the other things that are wrong with me later. Deal?"

I thought for a second and agreed. We pulled up at his house and he opened the door.

"Can you take a seat in the kitchen please?" he asked politely. As I entered the kitchen he bypassed me and went into his home office and came back with a disk in his hand. "While I went to pick you up this was burning." He placed the disk in the player and pressed play.

I couldn't believe what I was watching! Ray recorded the night he'd told me about with Tina and Girl X. I watched as Tina poked holes in the condoms and as Ray got naked and put on a show. I also watched as he exited the room after not touching a hair on her body. When the screen went black I said, "I apologize. I didn't believe you. So why were you with them when I saw you that day?"

"I had Tanya bring Tina to me for a little meeting. I told you that girl is a piece of work, so I made sure to give myself a little insurance, just in case. I popped the memory stick into the screen in my car and played it for her. I told her that if she ever tried to pull any slick shit I had proof of everything and I wasn't afraid to use it."

"Um...Ray...what is that?" I said pointing at the screen. Apparently, Tina wasn't the only woman on that tape. The date stamp on the video was only two days after their ménage and there was Girl X aka Tanya. He had her leaned over the desk and penetrated her from behind. The sounds from his office were muffled by the hustle and bustle of the busy office employees on the other side of the door. The secretary opened the door and discovered Raymond in a most precarious position. "Oh! Oh! Oh! Sorry," she said placing the file folder over her eyes.

"Close the door please." Raymond requested and returned to stroking his lady friend.

"Ok," Ray said holding his hands up. "There is really no good explanation for that one but we are just friends and I was really super pissed at you. But I never slept with Tina."

My blood boiled as I screamed obscenities at him before hearing the doorbell ring. I thought I might have been too loud and caused a neighbor to come by to check on Ray. When Ray opened the door, there stood Detective Rowe and two other officers.

"Are you Raymond Humphrey?" Bryant asked showing his badge.

"Yes, I am. What's this about?" Ray questioned.

"I need you to come with us," he said as he handed Ray the warrant.

As Ray began to read it he advised the officers that they must have made a mistake. "This is my name but I know nothing of this offense."

"I'm sure you don't Mr. Humphrey but in the meantime I going to read you your rights and this officer is going to put these nice shiny bracelets around your wrists. I need you to place your hands behind your back." Just as Detective Rowe finished his sentence the very audible finish of Girl X engulfed the house. I hurried to turn the power off on the TV and emerged from the kitchen.
"Desiree?" Detective Rowe asked with a look of confusion.

"Hi Bryant. What's all this about? Why is he under arrest?"

"Your friend here runs a prostitution ring."

I nearly fainted when the last word left his lips but he ran to catch me. "What did you just say?"

"That's not true Desi! This is a mistake!"

"So what was that noise I just heard?" Bryant asked Raymond.

"That was none of your business but it most definitely wasn't anything in the realm of prostitution."

Bryant turned to look back at me, "What are you doing here? How do you know this cat?"

My face was flushed and I explained that we worked together and the noise he heard was a recording of my best friend stabbing me in the back.

"So to your knowledge, were any of these women aware that they were being recorded?" he questioned.

"Not to my knowledge," I answered honestly.

"Desiree!!!" Raymond squealed.

"Alright, I will just have to take that into evidence," the officers placed Raymond in the squad car and re-entered the house. "Leave nothing unturned," Bryant instructed.

"I think I need to go home Bryant. I don't know anything about this. I was just here as a guest."

"Ok, you do that. I'll call you if I need anything from you."

"Ok. Thanks. And if you don't mind, please don't mention this to my husband. I don't have anything to hide but I also don't want him to think I can't pick my friends either. You know how it is being the wife of such a prominent figure."

"No worries, Desiree, I mean Mrs. Taylor, if I'm anything, I am discrete."

"Thank you," I said again as I walked out of the house and called Tara to pick me up at the nearest intersection.

20
SMALL WORLD

Wesley sat at the bar at Smith and Wollensky and toasted himself with one tequila shot after another. Ray sat beside him marveling at the mess that had been made. Wesley bailed Ray out of jail and promptly took him to the bar. After the first three shots, Ray conceded and watched as Wesley downed six more.

"Hey man. I think you've had enough," Ray finally advised.

"Nah, I'm just getting started," Wesley replied with a raspy voice.

"Listen, I've had a long day and I'm ready to see my house."

"Just one more. Let's toast to your freedom and friendship."

"We've done that already. If you're not ready I'm taking your car and you can call a cab when you finally piss on yourself."

"Alright. Alright. You drive and I'll drink," Wesley laughed.

"Whatever. Let's just go. You can stay at my house tonight."

The pair approached the valet who retrieved Wesley's car. Ray tipped him and took his seat on the driver's side as Wesley clumsily fumbled his way into the passenger side. Once inside Wesley turned the volume up on the radio and promptly passed out. Ray repeatedly looked over at Wesley to ensure he was still breathing then returned to his thoughts of how he'd ended up behind bars. *Who the fuck made such a big mistake? I've never done anything in my life to be arrested,* he thought. *On prostitution charges nonetheless!* As he turned into his driveway, Ray suddenly wished I'd came back and was there to greet him. He made up his mind to call once inside. Ray placed the car in park and slapped Wes' arm, "We're here. Get up!"

Wesley opened the car door and stood long enough to let the night air hit him before walking inside. He followed the sound of Ray's voice telling him to make himself comfortable, when he stopped in his tracks. With a dropped jaw, Wes simply pointed to the canvas painting on the wall. Ray turned around to notice his reaction and said, "Oh...that? Beautiful isn't she?"

"Why do you have that - I mean her, plastered on your wall like that?" Wes said finally able to speak.

"Yes. I know. That's her. That's Desiree. The woman I told you about."

"Yeah...I-I...don't you think this is a little fatal attraction scary?"

"Not one bit," Ray said walking into the kitchen. "She already saw it. It's art; like the Mona Lisa," he said returning with a glass of water and handed it to Wes.

"How did she see it? You've been seeing her again?" Wes said swallowing the water and staring at the portrait. It was a stunning piece of work and the detail was magnificent.

Ray smiled and nodded. He took a seat on the sofa that rested directly in front of it, crossed his legs, leaned back and extended each arm atop the back of the sofa. While shocked Wesley tried to play it cool.

"You do realize I *do* know this woman."

"You do?" Ray questioned sitting up, "How?"

"That's James Taylor's wife. We work together."

"Oh shit!" Ray said covering his mouth. "Small world."

"Man! What has gotten into you? First you had her spending the night here and now this! You're losing your playa card," Wes said taking another sip of water.

"How did you know she stayed here?" Ray's forehead scrunched as he tilted his head.

Wesley stopped drinking the water and said nothing for a moment. "You told me," he finally responded, trying to sound convincing.

"No. I'm sure I never told anyone that."

"You forget half the women you sleep with but you're sure you never told me that. Bruh c'mon," Wesley deflected.

"That may be true but I *know* I *never* told you that," Ray said moving to the edge of his seat. "How did you know that? I'm not going to ask you again."

"Calm down," Wesley said quickly sobering up. "I'll be straight with you."

"Yeah, you might want to try that shit for a

change," Raymond said as he stood up and folded his arms across his chest.

"Okay. I did know who she was because I came by awhile back unannounced to tell you about something I was getting into and I saw you meet her at the door," Wesley paused to observe the expression on Ray's face, which was quickly becoming a scowl.

"Seeing someone at my door and knowing that they were an overnight guest are two different things Wes. What else do you know and how do you know it?" Ray questioned.

After a long pause, Wesley opted to continue with his tail of deceit. "Look, there is a lot I didn't tell you and with good reason," he said as he took a seat on the arm of the brown leather chair near the window. "So here it is; I know her name is Desiree Taylor and that she's the wife of a colleague at the firm I work for. I also know you've been seeing her ever since her husband had a little play date or two." He paused again only to see Ray's jaw tighten. "I know you've got it bad for her and I can easily see why."

"We're supposed to be friends. Why didn't you say anything?"

"Like what? I figured if you wanted me to know you'd tell me. Clearly you didn't."

"My business is my business and *this* woman *is* my business," Ray pointed at the portrait.

"I know. That's why I never said a word. Soon enough she'll be yours once I'm done with her husband," Wesley replied with a smirk.

Ray, forgetting about the initial question,

turned his focus on Wesley's last statement. "What are you talking about?"

"I'm saying I think I've got enough on James to make life miserable for him and once that happens it's like a domino effect. Consider it an added bonus for a friend."

"Wait. Wait. What?" Ray said in an attempt to process what was happening. "Hold on, so that means when I told you about the altercation at Smith and Wollensky, you already knew who I was talking about?"

"Yeah," Wesley's cocky reply made Raymond pause. "I saw him shortly after, too." Wes continued with a laugh.

"So what is it that you have against this man?"

"It's a dog eat dog world," Wesley responded.

The pit of Ray's stomach started to churn as he searched Wesley's face. Suddenly things started to make sense; coincidences were no longer coincidences. Ray excused himself and retreated to his bedroom, telling Wesley to let himself out whenever he was ready.

21
SCANDAL

It had taken me a few days to process what happened to Ray. *A prostitution ring?* I couldn't even wrap my head around it. When Tara picked me up, ironically from a street corner I was barely able to get it out. Why is my life always so up and down when Raymond Humphrey is involved? *Why?* I was anxious and so I asked Tara to stay with me for a few days. Like the great friend she always is, she fussed at me about all the things she had to do, which I had an answer for of course; and went home to get an overnight bag.

I fixed dinner and chilled two bottles of wine in the freezer, one for her and one for me. We sat in the living room to eat and talked about everything else except what happened and why. Finally, I blurted out, "I've always been honest with myself, so I can admit when I'm wrong and I think I've done a good job of that so far." I took a sip from my glass. "I used to believe that there was nothing to explain about Tina. She does what she does and never apologizes for it. What for? I used to believe that people didn't understand that about her, which again, is why I made no excuses for her. She's the type of person that tended to get under people's skin and I liked that about her. I trusted that, depended on it. However, I don't pretend to know or even understand who that woman was that showed up in the church house acting all kinds of ugly that Sunday morning? Or who that woman was that was poking holes in Ray's condoms. Whatever demon that was that showed up is now spending time nursing a bruised ego, eye and jaw."

"I'm sorry, come again?" Tara said placing her glass on the table.

"Which part?"

"*Uh* the part about Ray and the condoms. I know about the church. Hell *everybody* knows about that fight at the church. I think there's a video of it floating around the internet for God sake."

"I don't even know where to start. I'm still processing. Don't get me wrong Tina is a beautiful person on the outside but uglier than ugly on the inside," I began.

"Please know that we only tolerated her because of you, Desi. I've never liked her and can honestly say I've never understood what you liked about her. But if you saw something good in her then I figured I must be missing something," Tara confessed.

"I know. Like I said, I liked that she was who she was all the time. I thought she gave me balance. Turns out I was wrong." I took another sip. "You know she actually told me once that between the two of us she was the 'star'. I just brushed it off because I knew she liked attention," I admitted.

"Come on, D! You let that slide?"

"I know. I know. I fed into her insecurities. But that was only because she told me so much about her past that I just felt like she needed someone there for her; to lift her up. She once told me that there was a time when she used to think that she was the most hideous creature alive. But one day she discovered it wasn't her, it was everyone else. So that's why she made the decision to not give a shit about anyone else's feelings anymore. And I respected her honesty. I just didn't think she would do that to me."

"What happened? How did you end up at Ray's house?"

"Okay, so you know how I told you that I saw her with that girl and Ray?"

"Yeah."

"Well Ray and I have been in communication with each other recently and --"

"What do you mean communication?"

"We've been talking to and seeing each other."

"Please don't tell me you slept with that man again."

I looked down at my glass and back at her, "Then I won't tell you."

"Desiree!" she shrieked hitting me with a pillow from the sofa.

I took a deep breath and released it. "I don't know what I was thinking. I just....I don't know. It just happened. I was trying to bring closure to the entire situation and one thing led to another."

"Does he know?"

"Know what?"

"About the embryo incident."

"Yes. I finally told him. That's how we got

on Tina. We basically argued about everything and I accused him of sleeping with her and he said he had proof that he didn't. That's when he showed me the video."

"*Video?* He taped them having sex?"

"Well he taped the event but he didn't have *actual* sex with her. He used a sex toy on her. But before any of that, he has her on tape poking holes in the condoms in his drawer when he and that girl left the room. I was disgusted by the whole thing."

"That's just scandalous!"

"I know! Then the tape continued and guess who was caught having sex on the same tape two days later with that girl? Yep. Ray!" I nodded.

"*No!*"

"The other girl apparently came back for more and he decided to record that too."

"Tina knew we were having an intimate relationship *and* she was with me when I found out I was pregnant with his baby. Somehow, even after knowing all of that she still thought it was a good move to try to sleep with him too."

"With friends like that, you don't need enemies. But Desi, something concerns me about all of this. If he was recording them without *their* knowledge, what if he has recordings of you without *your* knowledge?"

"Ray wouldn't do that," I said suddenly shaken.

"D, he was just arrested for prostitution. *Pro-sti-tu-tion.* What if you come up on some video? What if James finds out?"

"Oh my God, Tara! Oh my God!"

22

GIGGLES IN THE PARK

Lady K sat patiently on a park bench reading a book. She was dressed in a muted earth tone wrap with jeans and a pair of slippers and dark tinted sunglasses. She periodically looked up from her reading material to glance at her surroundings. The sun was bright in one direction so she used her hand as a visor. She looked to the left and back to her right where suddenly there stood Wesley.

"That must be one great read," he commented as he approached.

"It is but why do you say that?"she asked curiously.

"Because every time I see you, you've got it in your hands."

"What can I say, when I like something I go over it again and again. I like to make sure I didn't miss anything."

"Yet another reason to like you."

"I didn't know you had to find reasons," she said closing her book.

"Reasons are what keep me interested in you."

Lady K tried to contain her annoyance with her arrogant companion, "That's what I like about you Wesley, you're a straight shooter."

"Never a blank in the chamber," he smiled.

"Did you bring me anything?" she said changing the subject.

"Of course I did my darling," he handed her an envelope from his back pocket. "It's all there but I'm sure you're going to count it anyway."

"What businesswoman wouldn't count her money?" she said looking inside.

"I wouldn't expect anything less," he said placing his hands in his pocket and looking around. "You'll find your instructions for tomorrow laid out."

"Thank you. Now if you don't mind you're blocking my light," she said returning her attention to the novel. Wesley nodded and continued his slow stroll. He'd only walked about 25 yards before Lady K yelled, "Wes! Wait!" He stopped and turned with a wicked smile and her hurried pace caught up to him. "Look, now that we've concluded our business, well almost, I was thinking you could let me see how that mouth of yours really works," she said looking up at him with a seductive grin and giggled.

"I knew you'd come around to seeing it my way," Wesley replied.

"I'll admit I've been curious about you," she said tracing his chest with her finger. I've got some time this afternoon before my next meeting. Are you free?"

"I think I can squeeze you in."

"Follow me to my loft."

"After you, Madame," he said casually.

She walked in front of him until they crossed the park and landed at her sedan where he opened the door. Once inside Lady K looked at her own eyes in the rearview mirror, wondering if even she had balls enough to get through another moment with this man that she loathed so much. Her mental pep talk was interrupted when the corner of the mirror showed Wesley's car pull up behind her. They pulled away from the curb and onto the street. It was now or never. When they arrived at her loft, Wesley again opened her car door and extended his hand to assist her in getting out of the vehicle. "Thank you. I didn't realize you were such a gentlemen." she remarked. *Creep,* she said silently to herself and smiled.

"There is a lot you don't know about me," Wesley said smiling back and looking at her backside. He felt the lower half of himself swell ever-so-slightly. She felt his eyes on her back and noted that her body was gave and unexpected reaction. She swayed her hips a little more as she walked up the stairs toward the second landing and stopped. She turned to face her prey and to her surprise was met by softer wanting eyes.

Her hesitation to speak noticeably startled her. "I usually don't do this..." she started, "but there is something about you that just...just intrigues me." She said before kissing his lips as he stood one stair lower.

"I can honestly say the same about you," he said sincerely before kissing her back. They continued the walk to the third landing where she opened the door to a simple yet beautifully decorated exposed brick loft space. As Wesley entered, he realized that she'd brought him to her home and not a secluded brothel space like he'd imagined.

"Take your coat off while I get freshened up," she said placing her wrap on the corner of the couch. The space was open and the ceilings were tall. The art work on the wall was all black and white with hints of red accents throughout. There was a picture on a tall end table that rested against the back of the sofa; it was of her and what appeared to be her grandmother. It was the only picture of actual people in the place. Wesley studied it for a moment then looked around the place quickly before Lady K reentered the room wearing nothing.

To his surprise she walked right up to him, shoved her tongue in his mouth and gave the most mouth watering kiss he'd ever felt in his life. She then took his hand and led him over to the queen sized bed resting between two windows. She pushed him down and he fell willingly. His frame landed on the pillow top mattress with ease and he immediately began kicking off his shoes, unbuttoning and unzipping his pants. She took one finger and licked it before placing it between the folds of her virtue and tasted it. "You want to try it?" she asked squeezing her thighs together. Wesley nodded. Lady K walked around to the side of the bed as Wesley's eyes followed her and stopped just about where his head rested. She climbed onto the bed and straddled his shoulders backwards.

Her ass checks rested on his cheeks as she rode his face from the back. He managed to follow her rhythm with a stretched and tilted neck while he hastily removed his clothing; he was naked from the waist down with his socks still on. His dick flopped about but continuously firmed with each stride. She was moving from the waist down mostly. The sensation shot through her body like a volt of lightening when Wesley grabbed both butt cheeks and adjusted her so he could use his tongue to attack her anus. She leaned forward to escape; she had to keep control of this situation, so she reversed her position and took hold of the headboard. He stared up at her as she looked down upon him and let out a delicious moan.

Wesley could hardly contain himself. He placed his hands on her hips and moved her body down so that her yoni was now on his stomach. He could feel the flow of wetness pool there as her panting slowed and rolled her over on her back. He looked at her as if he was challenging her to stop him. It felt decadent. Her bent legs fell to either side. His penis dangled between her legs and with each swing it tapped her center and continued to harden. Just the touch of its head to her pearl alone made her inner tunnel stream with liquid and heat. The pulse of her clit was increasing. The anticipation of his steel entering her was enough to make her nipples perk and another moan escaped her lips. She placed the palm of her hand around the base of his head and pulled his neck toward her face. She shoved her tongue into his mouth once more. He pulled back and asked if she had a condom nearby, she pointed to a little drawer above her head inside the headboard. He pulled out the small silver knob and a drawer the size of a small jewelry box opened; he took one out and placed it over his wood.

He entered her intently from the missionary position with her legs bent in the air around him. Wesley couldn't help it. He looked at his strokes below as her climax reached its boiling point. She held his arms; elbows bent to her chest and her wrist wrapped his elbows with her hands and fingers gripping the fold of his arms. *Was Wesley making love?* she thought with a giggle. The shock of their obvious chemistry baffled her momentarily. Her legs trembled as she tried to compose herself enough to say something.

"You are...amazing!" he confessed. "That was better than anything I ever thought it would have been."

"You're not so bad yourself," she said stroking his chest. "Don't you have a meeting to get to?"

"Yes. But give me a few minutes and we can go another round."

Lady K chuckled at the invitation, "I have a meeting myself so I will have to take a rain check."

"I will cash it in very soon," he said as he got up and went into the bathroom.

"There's a fresh towel in the cabinet. Leave it on the side of the bathtub when you're done," she directed with a raised voice.

"Ok. Thanks!"

Wesley redressed himself and kissed her on the cheek and before saying a goodbye he said, "See you tomorrow my dear," with a wink.

"I'll be waiting for your call," she said blowing him a kiss.

No sooner did the door close did she run over to the window and wait for his car to pull away from the curb before she promptly called James. "Tomorrow is the day. Be ready," she said and hung up the phone.

23

THE BIG REVEAL

The boardroom was packed that morning with share holders, partners, and juniors. It was the quarterly meeting and the day the company would announce promotions. Everyone chatted about new plans and what growth would mean for the firm. Wesley entered James' office and asked if he was ready for the big day.

"Yeah. I think it's been a long time coming," James said with a straight face.

"Oh yes it has!" Wesley responded excitedly.

"I think you're in for a big surprise. I hear you've been busy making moves around here."

"Some, but not enough to cast a shadow of over the golden boy," Wesley said trying to sound comical. "Let's get up there before they start without us."

"Alright, I'm right behind you," James said grabbing a file from his drawer.

When the pair entered the room an applause went around. "Welcome gentlemen! Now that you're here we can get started," one of the partners said. Shortly after a discussion of profits and plans the time had come for the promotions announcement. Wesley sent a message for security to escort Lady K upstairs and to the boardroom. He sat poised and ready in his chair as he awaited the name James Jones Taylor to be announced. The chairman asked James to stand and make a statement.

"Greetings everyone. I would like to thank you for the opportunity to be considered for such a position. It has been my pleasure to serve this firm in my current capacity....which is the reason that I've also declined such a fantastic opportunity." James stopped to survey the reaction on each person's face. "I was told by both partners, whom I consider mentors and friends, that if I am not ready to take on such a task I must be confident enough to make the decision that is best for this firm and myself. Therefore, I've nominated someone else and I'm proud to say that nomination has been accepted; Wesley." James looked at him seriously, "Everyone please stand and congratulate our newest partner nominee." James clapped.

The blood drained from Wesley's face and he slowly stood and watched Lady K enter the room. Wesley looked to her then back at James. Then James looked over at her and back at Wesley as he rushed around the table with an, "Excuse me for a moment."

"Wesley! You sly devil! You must have known all along. Please, allow your girlfriend to stay."

"That won't be necessary. I will just see her out."

"No need to be embarrassed. We already know who she is and what she does for you." James said smugly.

"Come again?" Wesley asked.

"Once I nominated you for partner we had to confirm you. Make sure you were ready. That means we had to do some investigating to be sure you weren't going to add any blemishes on the firm's spotless record. I gladly volunteered to assist."

Wesley looked around the room, "I see."

James smiled. "Would you like to say anything Madame?"

Lady K walked over to James and handed him a drive. "It's all on here," she said with a wink. James placed the drive inside a port on a laptop sitting on the conference room table, connected to a projector. "Hit the lights for me please." All of the conference room guests' eyes widened as bits and pieces of recorded conversations between Wesley and Lady K played on the screen. The discussion of how to set James up was cut to eliminate any actual mention of the fact that they'd actually engaged each other. Video ended with the visual of Wesley having sex with a known Madame; Lady K and he had exchanged cash in the park.

She walked back over the Wesley and said, "No refunds. All sales are final," before turning up the lights again. Wesley stood for a minute as beads of sweat pursed his forehead. Animal instinct kicked in and he rushed toward James. The men in the room pulled him back as James made one final declaration, "I will never bring shame or scandal on this firm with such scrupulous actions and downright underhanded manipulations. If a man will do this to his own house...well you get where I'm going. That being said, if it pleases the board I would like to formally accept the nomination and confirmation of the partner position."

The chairman of the board stood to speak, "James Jones Taylor, the vote is unanimous, and you are confirmed! Security, remove this man from the premises. We will mail any personal belongings to you. If you will do that to one of our own...what's next, murder for hire?"

"Always play the fox. They'll never know you're the sanest man in the room," James said to Wesley on his way out.

"Have a nice weekend chairman," Lady K whispered on her way out of the door; his face flushed.

The room was abuzz with the happenings of the last few minutes before James excused himself. He had to find his Desiree! And he found me. And he found Ray.

24

LOVE VS HATE

My session with Dr. Anirbas went so well that I requested another hour. I told her about my most recent dream. I don't sleep much. There is too much stuff going on inside my head. I dreamt that Ray watched me have sex with J.J. He smiled at me when I noticed he was watching and when I closed my eyes and opened them again I was having sex with Raymond and James was watching and smiling. It woke me up in a panic.

As we sat and discussed my life in greater detail than I'd ever shared with another living soul she made a statement that resounded in my spirit; it was a real wake up call. She said, "Just because someone desires you, doesn't mean they value you." Those words echoed in my head for what seemed like another hour before I finally came to the conclusion that I was just as toxic or poisonous to Ray as he was to me. He *had* to protect himself. I never thought someone would need to be protected from me. I guess....I guess *he* did. We've all done damage. If you put yourself in the other person's shoes, one person's damage is not greater than the others. It's about perspective.

"I want to stop doing this," I said sharply.

"Doing what Desiree?"

"All of this back and forth with Raymond and James. I want to stop this now." The heavens opened up and heard me; it was time to end this. While the tears flowed, I felt a weight lift off my shoulders. All I could think of was how much I wanted the best life for him and myself and how much I would love to be friends. *Real friends.* Since we can't take any of this back, we could at least appreciate the journey. I deserved some of this. I did. It was time to go home. It was time to repair myself and my marriage.

The man who devoted his life to me was still waiting for me to get my act together. The man who'd pick up the phone without hesitation every time I called was waiting for me. The man who made it his business to learn me and be there for me was awaiting my return. "I hope this goes well," I said aloud. "You know, it's funny.... your love doesn't mean a thing when you say good night to one person and good morning to another."

My drive home was nothing short of a daze. My mind weighed the pros and cons of both James and Raymond; the good, bad, and worst possible scenarios with each man. I was so involved in my mental list I passed my house only to circle around and pass it up again. Once I gathered myself enough to focus, I parked the car and began sobbing. The tears came from out of nowhere. *What am I doing to myself; to my life? Why am I actually considering a relationship with a man that turned is back on me when I needed him most! A man that I caught with my best friend of all people, the choice should be easy. Right?* My husband made a mistake. A *really* big life altering mistake but a mistake nonetheless. My husband didn't come after me lustfully he came after me with love and repentance in his heart. The choice should be easy. *Right?*

∞ ∞ ∞

Ray and I sat in his living room having an unofficial staring contest. We were both searching for where to begin but neither of us had ever been in a situation like this before. So it appeared the winner got to speak first. He finally took his gaze away from mine so I spoke, "Have you ever tried to stop messing with me?" I asked seriously.

"I tried. It didn't work," Raymond answered seriously. "I've waited for so long just to be with you."

"I know you have."

"It's time to make a decision."

"I know you need one."

"So what's it gonna be?"

"Ever since the two of us have gotten together things have been a mess. One thing I know for sure and two things I know for certain; I love you deeply. I truly do. Are you the man for me? No. Are you the man I'm supposed to marry? No. A real relationship has its ups and downs but this one has had too many to successfully repair. You slept with my friend - well almost." I paused to stop his objection. "And like I said, I don't want to hurt anybody but everybody is getting hurt in the process. Maybe you will never understand the bond between a husband and wife and that's okay but I do and I know I owe it to James to make this right once and for all."

"You don't have to be married to know what it's like to care about somebody deeply, Desi."

"See, that's it right there....You want an old school love...and I can give that to you but you're trying to get it using new school tactics and games, Ray."

"Now that's the best joke I've heard all day!" Ray said sarcastically. "Desi, this whole thing is your fault because you're the married one. So I guess that means since you're here with me that you don't know what the hell you want."

"What is that supposed to mean?!"

"Because you're not supposed to be here, that's what!" Ray snapped. "No obligations. And as for that husband of yours, he shouldn't know anything about me!"

"So you're saying you don't love me?"

"What's not to fall in love with? You're everything." His tone drastically shifted and alarmed me.

"All I know is that there are two men, and one doesn't belong," I said in a failed attempt to remove any emotion from the conversation.

"You know what, at the end of the day you should have told your husband what you really wanted. Every man wants to be the first at something sexually, especially with the woman he really loves. But it's cool, go ahead and be the whore you really are," Ray said with cold eyes before he began mumbling to himself. "Just should've fuckin' told him. Should've never messed with a married women. That's where I went wrong."

"How did we go from did you love me to *this*?" I asked angrily.

"Yes! I loved you! I loved fucking you," he said in response. Ray knew that wasn't at all the truth of the matter but he wanted me to hurt. He wanted his words to linger and sting.

I saw that...I saw him for the first time and I couldn't breathe. "Now would probably be a *really* good time to shut your mouth before I start hating you."

"I don't care!" Ray's words were wounded.

"Shut your fuckin' mouth!" I yelled and got up with a raised hand. We were both standing on the edge of madness and we were both about to jump all because Ray was tripping over his own ego.

"You can't be mad. I don't understand how you can get mad! You're married!" he yelled back as he caught my hand in the air from slapping his face.

"Seeing you in that video with that girl doing all those freaky things....you're disgusting!"

"I don't care. I don't care! I *don't* care....." Ray said then paused, "I do care," he admitted defeated. "I feel like you played with me and that really hurt me because I really do have strong feelings for you and I just don't want you to lead me on and you really don't have those type of feelings for me."

"I can admit this was a bad decision."

"You'll miss me again, but next time I won't be back. You've lost me for good this time."

"I know...it's too late....You said you loved me but you left. Do you have any real feelings at all?"

"For what? For You? You're not who I thought you were."

"I love you. I love spending time with you but what do you think we're doing here? Playing house?"

I was too much in my own emotions to see any logic in what he was saying. It was foolishness pure and simple. There was no rhyme or reason to any of this! I was there with him, not playing house, at least in my eyes. I was there with him being who and what he needed me to be when he needed it. I was showing him I was his for the taking. Somewhere along the way he apparently saw it the opposite. To him I was playing house, I wasn't his for the taking and I damn sure wasn't his wife; that title belonged to James. This was his way of protecting himself...from...*me*. I never thought he needed protecting. Too many hurt feelings were exchanged and too much had happened between us. Too many lies had been told and possibly way too much sex had been exchanged. I stopped my rage instantaneously and asked Ray if he could understand that I do love him and that was not a game or a lie.

"I don't want to hate you," Ray said releasing me.

"Hate is a strong word," I came back.

"So is love," he reminded me before turning

his back.

"You're right," I said defeated. We hugged for what seemed like an eternity. The longer we hugged the tighter he held me and the more I cried. I cried for the experience. I cried for the loss and I cried for us.

"You know I really do love you! And it hurts beyond words that this is ending the way it is."

"I'm almost relieved that this happened."

"Why?"

"Because you've made it that much easier for me to let you go. I love you but I love me more. I thought I would have to make a harder decision but right now I've never been so clear."

"If at this hour you have no love for me, I don't need you to stay," he said looking into my eyes. At that moment I needed a serious breakdown from all of this. I couldn't take it. Ray and I are complicated. We loved each other to madness and neither would admit to not truly trusting the other.

Ray and I stood face to face, eyes locked, mentally daring the other to make the first move. I was in a state of personal panic but did my best to appear calm, cool and collected. I wanted him in the worst way physically but couldn't help wonder if emotionally I was daring myself to use him as an escape from the real problem. I'd thought the decadent thrill of seduction between Ray and I had disappeared until now. I knew he didn't deserve me and I also knew I didn't deserve James.

So there we were at a crossroads, playing a dangerous game of chicken, when Ray took matters into his own hands. He reached for me and I slightly swiveled backwards. He never took his eyes off of me as he reached for me again, this time with both hands. He began stroking my arms up and down in the most soothing rhythm. His eyes asked for permission to move with a glance at my shoulder. I looked in the general direction and back at him; the answer was yes. I felt like a teenager exploring sexuality for the first time. Just as I did back then, I stood here now with an angel on my right shoulder saying, "Don't do it," and a devil on my left shoulder saying, "Just one more time. It won't hurt." I couldn't shake the feeling that disaster was near. Temptation...oh the temptation, to taste and feel all that I'd been missing; the passion.

Ray's fingers were busy pulling down the straps of my tank top and bra. He managed to help my arms out of each restraint so may bare breasts were fully exposed and hardening at each passing moment. He continued to wrap his arms around my upper body and unsnapped my bra. It fell to the floor and I breathed deep; I guess the heaving of my chest was just the invitation he needed. I felt the heat of his tongue on my lips as he circled them and entered softly. I felt myself cum just a little. Ray's subtle caress made me weak. My body confirmed with a small gush of wetness that rested between the fold of my yoni and another when I felt his hands cup both of my breasts as he continued to kiss me with such tenderness. He liked to ride my curves and I felt the love and care in his touch and his kiss.

The angel on my right began to change her tune. She went from saying, "Don't do it," to "Oh my! This *is* real. He really does love you." And the devil went from saying, "One more time." to "Wrong can be right." So I reciprocated by placing my palms on his pecks and closing my eyes and kissing him. I felt an overwhelming sense of warmth between us, almost like we needed each other; like we needed to do this. We needed to be sure this wasn't just phenomenal sex that kept us coming back. I felt secure, sexy, and sweet under his spell. *This is how I should feel every day.* I raised his soft cotton v-neck over his head and tossed it on the floor. He kissed me harder. He grabbed my face with both hands and for a moment it seemed as though he wanted to devour me but ultimately decided against it. He stepped back to look at me and finally spoke, "If you want to stop, I will understand. But for the record, I don't. I'm ready."

"I'm not." I said without hesitation. Our day of reckoning had come. That comment, I'm ready, tripped a light inside my head. I knew he wasn't talking about sex; he was talking about he and I being in this together. He was talking about a relationship. My head began to settle as those words exited my lips and I stepped toward Ray and placed a single kiss on his lips. I started for my bra and he caught my hand and picked the bra up for me. "Let me," he said sincerely. He picked up the black, satin and lace bra and began to slowly redress me. He placed simple kisses to my lips with each snap placement. I watched in awe like an out of body experience as he put me back the way he found me.

"I want you to stay. We don't have to do anything. But Desi, please know how much I want you to stay."

"*Ummm*...okay," I said trying to gather myself. "I'm tired," was the only other thing I could say.

"Then let's lay," Ray said taking my hand in his and led me to the couch. He sat down and twisted himself so one leg rested on the couch and the other was bent so his foot was planted on the floor. He pulled me toward him and I found myself lying on my stomach in between his legs resting my head comfortably on his chest. Without another word, Ray rubbed my back until I fell asleep. It was one of the most memorable nights of my life. That's when I knew I was in love with two men. When I laid my head on his chest and I was there. I was home.

"Your body is here with me but your mind is on the other side of town."

"I officially hate you."

"Hate is such a strong word."

"Not when it's the truth. It's the right word if it fits the bill."

"No it doesn't because you don't mean that."

"Yes I do. I hate you with a passion!"

"Passion is love NOT hate."

"There is a thin line between love and hate."

"Yes but we haven't crossed it yet."

"When will this ever end?"

"When you decide it's over."

"Again with all the answers. I don't like you very much."

"That's because you love me," he said with a smile.

I lifted my head and shoulders from his lap and turned to look at him. I brushed his cheeks with my hand and smiled back, "I believe your eyes."

"Good because they are telling you the truth," he said pressing my body forcing it to return to its resting position. "You can still read them....Impressive."

I woke up satisfied but guilty as hell. Which one of them gets the best of me? Not everything in life is cut and dry. There are gray and even dark areas that sometimes require exploration. There are no guarantees in anything we choose but the fact is the choice is always yours. You may not like the outcome or the options but it's no one's fault but your own -- no matter *who or what* the variables are in your equation.

25

SEX AND DECADENCE

Now here we are. Here's James holding a gun on Raymond; my entire happy ending has been shot to hell, literally. In the beginning, I thought doing all of this would make me feel better. I thought getting back at James would make us even. It didn't. It made it worse but in some strange way it also made me better. I feel like a better woman. I feel like me. I feel like it taught me a lot about myself, about us, about life, about truth, about being honest. Like I said before, I'll never apologize for it. I take that back, I'd apologize for hurting the people I love but never for the experience and never for the things it has taught me.

As Raymond lay on the floor of his own home trying to figure a way out of this mess, he made a bold decision; he decided if he was going to die, he was going to go out with a bang.

"You and I both want your wife," Ray declared.

"The difference between you and me is I already have her. She *is* my wife!" James said threw gritted teeth.

"That can always be changed," Ray responded with confidence.

"Don't be so sure Mr. Humphrey. Things

aren't always what they seem." And with that James cocked the gun once more. "Game on!"

"Ray!" I shrieked bursting through the door and running over to his side. "Now is *not* the time to be cocky! James what are you doing?! Put that gun down!" I'd forgotten my purse at Raymond's house and went back to get it. To my surprise I noticed J.J.'s car and my stomach immediately sank. I jumped out of the car and looked through the window on the side of the door to find my husband pointing a gun at my ex-lover. What was the world coming too?!

The look on my husband's face was as if he was coming back to himself. He looked at me, "So was it all worth it?" he said before another loud *BANG* rang out! Instinctively I squeezed my eyes shut, screamed and did my best to shield Raymond's body. I waited to feel pain or a rush of fluid but nothing happened. I slowly opened my eyes to see the gun pointed away from us. James had shot the bullet in the chamber into the wall behind us. My heart raced and I couldn't stop crying.

"James, please," I said releasing Raymond and crawling over to him. All I wanted to do was hug him and told him, "Nothing could ever change the love I have for you. You didn't have to do this." I cried.

"I need you," he breathed deep. "I love you. I'm supposed to protect you."

"I don't need you to protect me I need you to support me, just like I supported you. We've got to fix this! He needs an ambulance J.J."

"I know. I know. But not before we get

something straight," James said moving away from me and over toward Ray. "Listen, since you've already created the perfect storm, I'll give you a choice right now and you better choose wisely. I can nail your ass to the wall for prostitution and about five other felonies including video voyeurism *or* when the police arrive you tell them that you have no idea who shot you and I will make sure *all* of those charges and *all* of the evidence disappears." James was so methodical. I'd never seen this side of him. "Oh and there is one other caveat, you stay away from my wife! Because if you don't all of those charges and evidence will find their way back into your life and into a courtroom and my star witness will be sure to have a nicely detailed account of how you ran your affairs."

∞ ∞ ∞

Have you ever discovered something about someone you're dating or married to that changed how you thought about them? The hardest thing I ever had to do was admit that I played a part in the demise of my marriage. The heat inside my face behind my nose and eyes burned until the water well behind my eyes gave way and released all of the tears that had been building up. My nose felt the sting with each tear that I tried to hold back until I swallowed hard and couldn't contain it any longer. My hands cupped my face as my body leaned forward. I could no longer pretend that everything was fine, that I was ok....that I had it all together. My chest heaved, my nose ran, and snorted like a pig...this was an ugly cry. The kind that makes you face puff and turn red....the kind that ages you physically but makes you feel years younger once your done.

"If you wanted something real it was right here waiting for you to make up your mind. You either don't want it or you weren't ready. Either way I made the decision for the both of us. Why do you keep coming back? Why are you here?" James said somberly as he sat on the couch next to me.

"I don't know why you did what you did. I wasn't enough? All you had to do was talk to me. You made choices and so did I. My choices brought this because of my gender but your choices could have ended the same way," I said squeezing my stomach. "I tried to understand...I tried to give you the space and love you needed but you took that for granted."

"You had your fun and I had mine. That's all in the past now. We've both made mistakes." James responded.

"No. No. No, J.J. this wasn't fun. This was my life! Not a game!" I said turning to face him. He could not answer.

∞ ∞ ∞

Time flew by; all of those days, weeks and months until they became my past imperfections. No one existed here. Just me. Only me. Smiling through all the rain and the pain reminds me of this cold and wet feeling you get when you unhunch your shoulders while walking in the rain. Then you realize that the cold is not a bad thing but a calming one. The wetness is not icky but comforting and the pressure of the sky shower is actually a way for GOD to massage your pain away. That's where I'm at now. That's the place where I want to stay for awhile. It feels good here. Things become clearer here, even with the down pour. I'm smiling in this place. Where I feel alive again. Yes! Alive again! Thank GOD for the rain and the pain! After all this...good morning.

"How was your vacation?" Dr. Anirbas asked as I made myself comfortable.

"Long ago and far away," I said without hesitation.

"You're sad. You're weak. This is your chance for a fresh start."

"It doesn't take much to reason why I did what I did. Whatever I wanted was mine for the taking and I had the perfect excuse," I said with revelation. "I asked God to take away my desire for him. I prayed as hard as I could. You know what I've come to realize? Ray did lose but none of us won."

"Life is full of surprises," She simply replied. "The trick is remembering; don't get in your own way."

I chuckled at such a sentiment before responding, "I chose the road of passion and pain. I took back my soul. But the funny thing is you're going to be the one that saves me...from me."

"You say that with such decadence."

"Decadence: Such a powerful word with almost little to no meaning for most who've never really experienced it. I've tasted it. In fact I've devoured it to the point of total annihilation. My own person sexual revolution. Basically my moral decline. My decay. Funny I wouldn't have called it a decline or decay a few months ago. More like revenge. Except I'm still recovering from all of my...decadence. I like that word. It's sexy and packs a mean punch! Yep! That about sums it up: Sex and decadence," I said with certainty to my therapist. "We are all sexual beings. At least that's the way I see everyone. No matter what's going on in life it boils down to some form of sex. You know how people tell you to imagine everyone in the room naked to get over your fear of speaking - that's what I do except I pay attention to details when I imagine them naked if you know what I mean."

"If you're being honest with yourself, when you took that object and pierced your skin did you believe the feelings you thought you stabbed away are still there?"

The question shook me to my core. "The long and short of everything is simple. I will never apologize for doing what I've done and going through what I went through. I'm stripped to nothing and I don't care. I can't care. I have to find the silver lining in all this. And I think I'm on the brink of just that!"

"It becomes less and less about your sexuality and more and more about the person. That's love."

"It ain't all roses. Sometimes you have to wake up and smell the thorns," I chided. "Beat. Beat. Beat, goes the heart in those moments in time where life gives you drama and pauses. I can't tell if I'm on a beat or a pause moment. Guess I'll just have to wait and see what happens next to decide," I shrugged.

Dr. Anirbas took a deep breath and said, "Recovery is going to take some time, Desi. I think we should start from the beginning. You mentioned a tragedy when you were younger. Tell me about your brother, Derrick Pender."

EPILOGUE

There was something about his touch. Something in the way he placed his hands on my hips and rested them there. Always my hips, never my waist.

"Where is everybody?"

"What everybody? It's just me and you."

COMING SOON!

Those Necessary Thorns: Derrick Pender

Written by Sabrina Childress
Story by Aretha Cephus

Before James Jones Taylor and Raymond Humphrey, there was Derrick Pender, Desiree Elizabeth Taylor's baby brother. This is the story of how a major tragedy changed her life. The moment when Desiree learned that eyes really are the soul.

Derrick Pender was the innocent unborn child of Phillip and Ester Rose Pender before their divorce. He came into a world where jealousy reigned supreme and the ultimate price was paid with his life.

"All things truly wicked start from an innocence."
Ernest Hemingway

ABOUT THE AUTHOR

Sabrina Childress is a graduate of Columbia College in Chicago. Sabrina has managed a dual career in public relations as well as the not-for-profit sector through the founding of Position of Pressure nfp, a grassroots domestic violence organization for teens and young adults.

Often described as a paradigm shift, Sabrina writes books about. struggles, temptations, human nature, and the triumphs of relationships, perceptions, and expectations. As an author, Sabrina likes to challenge others to deal with the real issues of being human.

Follow @TNTBook
Visit www.TNTBook.com

What If....

By

J. Will

Jackie walked to the front door and looked through the peephole to get a glimpse of her visitor. She was surprised to see who was standing on the other side. Turning to the mirror in her foyer, she did a quick once-over. Jackie rubbed her hands over her long ponytail to smooth it out. Her chocolate skin was smooth and clad in comfy sweats and a tank top. She admired her tall frame and tiny body. Remembering how often she'd been told she'd be perfect for modeling, Jackie took a deep breath, turned the knob and opened the door. He stood in front of her as she took a moment to just take him all in. Jackie always had a thing for guys with a jock build, especially the tall ones. Six foot four inches of golden caramel skin, he definitely fit her criteria.

"Bryan, what are you doing here?"

"I came to see you. What do you mean?"

"I wasn't expecting you. No call or text, and you know I don't do surprise visits. Do I just show up at your house?"

"You could if you wanted to." The look on her face said 'yeah right' as she turned to walk away.

"Please, you would love that."

"Babe, what's the problem? I thought you would be happy to see me."

"Who says I'm not?"

"Well you don't act like it."

Jackie stopped in her tracks and turned to face him. "Bryan, now you know if things were different I would -"

"Jackie, I don't want to rehash this again. I came to see you, to see your smile which makes me smile, and to just relax before I go home." He said cutting her off.

"Mmhmm. Bryan you must have forgotten who you are talking to. Do not try to BS me. You came over here to get laid!"

"No, I came to see you, although that is always a bonus." Bryan flashed his pearly whites at her and gave her a quick peck on the lips.

"What makes you think you have a chance tonight?" Jackie asked with a smirk.

"Because you never tell me no." Bryan answered taking a step closer.

"LIES! Do not make me sound like that girl who is happy to have a piece of a man anyway she can have him because I am not that girl."

"Did I say you were?"

"That's how you're making it sound."

"Ok, that's not what I meant. What I meant is that we both know how irresistible I am. And you know that you want me." He reached out for her hand, pulling her into an embrace. Jackie loved how it felt when he wrapped his arms around her. Bryan's arms were big, not muscular, but almost toned. Whenever he hugged her like that, Bryan would always kiss the top of her head.

"Bryan,"

"Jackie." Bryan said as he let her go and interlocked their fingers. He turned and walked from the foyer, down the hallway and into the living room. Sports Center was playing on the 55 inch television screen resting on the wall. "Look at this;

you were waiting for me to come through." He led her to the couch where he sat down first and then pulled her gently to sit on his lap.

"You really need to get a grip."

"You look really good right now. You know I love you in sweats and a tank."

"It really doesn't take much to get you turned on."

"True. I missed you."

"Really?"

"Yes, I thought about you all day while I was at work. Why else would I just pop over here?"

"I don't know. Maybe you should tell me what you were thinking about."

"Nah, I'd rather show you." He smiled at her as he leaned over moved the hair out of her face. He kissed her like he was kissing her for the first time. He sucked on her bottom lip. Jackie softly moaned. Dripping with passion and desire, he cupped her face and took over her mouth. His kisses became harder when she suddenly stopped him.

"What's wrong?" The lust washed away from Bryan's face and was replaced with confusion and concern.

"Nothing, I just want to adjust my position." Jackie got up and straddled him. "Yes. Much better." This time Jackie struck first by giving Bryan hard kisses, biting his bottom lip before tracing the outline of his lips with her tongue. She knew that turned him. Bryan put his arm around her body and got up from the couch, headed to the staircase when she stopped him again.

"The wall." Bryan carried her over to the wall.

He use the wall the support Jackie's back. Jackie was definitely getting aroused and pulled Bryan to her by putting her arms around his neck and crossing her legs around his waist. Bryan stared into her eyes, calling her beautiful and kissed her. Before she knew it, he'd swiped her sweat pants right off. While she unbuckled his belt and pants, Bryan sucked on her neck; one of her spots. Pulling his attention back to her face, he cupped it and gave her tongue, juicy and wet. The moans coming from them almost sounded like they were competing against one another.

"Do you want me to stop and go home?"

"Really Bryan?"

"Tell me what you want."

"I want you to stop talking so you can slide in and out of me."

"Oh yeah? You mean like this?" He slammed himself inside of her wetness; it caught her off guard and she gasped. "Or do you want it like this?" He slid in nice and slow, watching her reaction. Jackie's eyes were closed and she was sucking in her breath.

"Babe, you know I don't like to be teased." Jackie's voice was soft spoken, her eyes still closed, moving with his movements.

"You know I do it to mess with you."

"Yes, that you do." She smiled and opened her eyes.

"I want you so much right now."

"What are you waiting for? Stop playing around."

"Ok." He used his right hand to hold on to her

and keep them both balanced. Her back arched against the wall. He met each kiss with a thrust and moved at different paces which he knew would drive her crazy. He loved teasing her, watching her wither against him, slapping his chest when he was getting too into his little game, growling at him while nibbling his ear and running her nails up and down his back.

He was getting closer and closer to his peak; she could tell by the glassy look in his eyes and his labored breathing. He was moving faster and faster, gripping her harder to keep her in place. Her legs locked around him as she was getting closer and closer to reaching orgasm. His strokes were long, but fast, penetrating her until he couldn't go any further. She made sure that she took him all the way in to maximize her pleasure. He went faster and faster. BUZZ! BUZZ! BUZZ! BUZZ! The alarm clock abruptly screeched.

Jackie was startled awake by the combination of the sound of her alarm and the sunshine that hit her face. She was not looking forward to this day at all. She out of her bed and walked over to the window to look outside. It was a picture perfect day, perfect day for a wedding but not hers. She had missed her chance and was unsure of ever getting a second chance. Picking up the wedding invitation and looking at it, she must have been a fool to even consider going let alone to RSVP. Who spends two months driving everyone around her crazy trying to find "the perfect dress" for your ex's wedding? Yes, she would look good today, but did it really matter in the end if Bryan married anyone but her?

She kept replaying their relationship in her mind, over and over like she was editing a movie. Ten years ago, they were a young, carefree couple that just couldn't make it work. She didn't think they had a future and he never showed his serious side to her. It wasn't until after they were broken up did she discover his true feelings. Keeping her distance from him was the best thing to do in her mind so that's what she did. But when they did see each other again, it was like nothing had changed. That is, until he told her that he was engaged.

Jackie felt a certain way about Bryan. She cared for him still and was protective of him. When they finally had the chance to sit and clear the air, she knew that there was still something between them. The attraction had always been there, the chemistry was great and they were compatible on so many levels. The last couple months were great but it also had her questioning her sanity and now she didn't know how she was going to get through this day.

While she was wrapped up in her thoughts and getting herself ready, she heard the doorbell ring. Now who could this be coming by unannounced on today of all days? She quickly unlocked and opened the door without even checking to see who was out there and was surprised to see him standing there. He was dressed in his tux, all white, from top to bottom and he looked damn good.

"Bryan, what are you doing here?"

"Jackie, I can't do it."

"Do what Bryan?"

"Jackie, I cannot marry her."

"What?"

"Last night I couldn't sleep thinking about us."

"Bryan, I think -"

"No, just hear me out. I kept thinking of what you said about marrying one person when you have another in your heart and I realized that I can't do it. I do not want to lose you, not again. I don't want to think about what you are doing and who you are with and wishing I could see you even though I have a wife. I want you to be my wife and you should have been my wife years ago. So Jackie Reese, will you marry me?"

Stay tuned....

ABOUT THE AUTHOR

J. Will is an up and coming author by day and superhero by night.

Follow me on Twitter @authorjwill

www.ingramcontent.com/pod-product-compliance
Lightning Source LLC
Chambersburg PA
CBHW021043130626
46552CB00005B/1999